Eugene Lee-Hamilton

Poems and Transcripts

Eugene Lee-Hamilton

Poems and Transcripts

ISBN/EAN: 9783337158330

Printed in Europe, USA, Canada, Australia, Japan

Cover: Foto ©Andreas Hilbeck / pixelio.de

More available books at **www.hansebooks.com**

POEMS AND TRANSCRIPTS

BY

EUGENE LEE-HAMILTON

TO

JOHN RUFFINI

THIS VOLUME

IS RESPECTFULLY AND AFFECTIONATELY

DEDICATED

CONTENTS.

I.—POEMS IN BLANK VERSE.

II.—ELEGIES.

III.—POEMS IN LYRICAL METRES.

IV.—TRANSCRIPTS.

I.

POEMS IN BLANK VERSE

A DWARF.

In the strong daylight of reality,
I came upon a being who belonged
Not to the present, but the distant past;
A thing mis-issued from the womb of Time,
Which called the mind away from present sights,
And seemed to give the measure of an age.
I saw him at Verona in the street;
And with that empty street, in which the sun
Poured floods of light upon the heated stones.
He seemed as out of keeping as a bat.
He was a cripple and a dwarf, of face
Close-shaven, warped, and pleasureless, who stood
Upon his crutches, in the dreary garb
Of a medieval almshouse, eyeing us.
He might have been an imp-like ornament,
Detached from some cathedral buttress black,
And vivified by now forgotten spells;
The incarnate spirit of the Ages Dark,
Thrown on our path to make us love these days.

I let my thoughts revert to those black times,
When prowled the monk, the leper, and the witch

Amid the rubbish of a nobler world;
When blunted was the mind by ignorance
And dull despair, and much the body, too,
Was stunted, and misshapen, and debased
By centuries of famine, when mankind
Were but a herd of mean and trembling slaves,
Beneath the lash of heaven, and their voice
A litany unceasing.   Then the Dwarf
Became the sculptor's model; and the more
Distorted and malignant was his face,
The more he served his purpose.   Everywhere
He leered from out the stonework, in the gloom
Of cloister and of church, where he sustained
The short and thick-set pillarets with pain
On his ignoble shoulders; or he peeped
With apish gobiins as a water-spout,
Over the belfry's brink, or crouched high up,
And seemed to jeer beneath the Gothic eaves;
And in the twilight, struck a sickening fear
In women's hearts, and made them oft, perhaps,
Give birth unto his like.   Had the pale sun
Not strength enough, in those ill-omened times,
To warm men's hearts to gladness, and a sense
Of human beauty?   Did not Nature speak?
And came no voices from the distant past?
No voices came, or, if they came, were faint.
In premature decrepitude, the world
Had little memory of its golden youth,
When held in honour was the human form,
And when, in Greece, the sculptor loved to mould
The youth still sprinkled with Olympic dust;
When Phidias and Praxiteles had clothed
Immortal Gods in Man's most beauteous shape,

And shown to all the Zeus of mighty brow,
The armed and placid Pallas, or the young
Triumphant Phœbus, in his radiant strength;
And her who rose from ocean's tossing foam,
Supremely fair; or happy leaf-eared Fauns,
O'er-filled with life, and fresh from woodland glades.
Those days were dead : the Gods of Hellas slept
Within the bosom of the patient earth ;
What was not dust was hidden in the dust,
And half a thousand years had still to pass
Before their waking day.   And even then,
When once again they stood in Heaven's light,
In their own grand serenity, how few
Were those whose hearts could recognise their rule,
Or give the disinherited their due !
Alas, alas ! for beauty's noblest world !

The Middle Ages, like a sea of lead,
Extend immense and desolate ; a sea
On which the sun appears for ever set,
And through the lasting twilight we perceive
Some few wrecks of Antiquity.   Look back
With me upon those times of woe, when first
The bell's dull tolling marked the close of day,
And rendered sadder nightfall's saddening hour.
The thousand woodland gods of Greece were gone :
The sunlit glades were empty, which had once
With joyous beings teemed.   But in the gloom,
In damp and chilly dells of evil name,
Where clumps of henbane and of monkshood grew.
A thousand other beings dwelt instead,
Spiteful and ugly, who on toadstools sat
And waited for the passer-by to cross

His path and bode him ill.   The dreaded Nix
Dwelt in the depths of sunless forest pools,
And lured the fisher, while the dwarfish Gnomes
Betrayed the miner in the caves of earth.
The world was peopled with fantastic shapes
Of ugliness and fear, which man, alas,
Had formed in his own image.   Fear and Hate
And Hunger reigned.   The lean and stunted serf,
Nailed to his clod of unproductive earth,
Looked at the frowning castle near at hand,
Whence came all desolations, and worked on
In silent hatred.   Near him, tall and black,
The gibbet stood against the leaden sky.
A sound of brutal revelry at times
Fell on his ear, or else a chaunt of monks,
Monotonous and soulless, from afar.
Unless the plague swept by and took him off
With his lean children, and with monk and lord,
He struggled on, and asked no human help.
But often, by the moon's precarious light,
Upon some wild, ill-omened heath, as bare
As the dead level of his misery,
He offered up a midnight mass to him
Who first rebelled.   The witch, his priestess, stood,
Not old and shrivelled, as some now might think,
But with an impious beauty in her face,
And black and snake-like locks, and braved aloud
All heaven's bolts.   The great satanic reel
Went ever faster, and the pale, chaste moon
Drew o'er her face a fleecy veil of cloud.

I love those ages not; but even they,
Barren and mean and cruel as they were

Have left us things of beauty. Then arose
The great cathedrals, which uplift the cross
Into the clouds, high o'er the hum of life.
See how the patient generations worked
For far posterity. They sought not fame,
But deemed that he would not have lived in vain
Whose hand had added to the glorious pile
An oriel window or a sculptured porch,
Though lost should be his name. The work was slow.
Full well they knew that ere the latest stone
Of dazzling white was laid, high in the sky,
The first would long have blackened been by age,
And unborn kings be sleeping in the crypt.
But year by year the marble forest grew ;
The Gothic columns, like gigantic sheaves
Of mighty rushes, higher, higher rose,
And spread, and bent, and met above the aisles
In loftiest arch, and took the tints of time,
While wondrous vistas formed, where, far away,
The softened light streamed through the stainéd glass.
Yes, even those cold ages, when men looked
So little on the beauty of the world,
Bequeathed us things of beauty which endure.
But that was when the long-retarded dawn
Already struggled with the night. For, lo,
A change was coming o'er the face of earth.

A change, indeed ; all nature's face was changed,
And rendered youthful in the eyes of men.
The trees, which for a thousand years had seemed
Like gibbets in a mist, took beauteous forms ;
The scentless flowers filled the air with scent,
And claimed their tints of yore. The dew-drops shone,

The ripened corn resumed its golden hue,
And through the world there passed a breeze of life.
See how Æneas Sylvius[1] takes delight
In the blue waving fields of flow'ring flax;
And thou, Lorenzo,[2] who didst note the charm
Of early winter in thy princely home
Of Ambra, where the dry and rustling leaves
Made, in the thinnéd woods, the steps of one
Sound like the steps of many; where the cranes,
In homeward flight, were printed on the sky;
Where still the cypress some few birds concealed.
What hand in painting nature equals thine?
For thee the Nereids sported as of old
Among the sparkling waters, and the Fauns
Lurked 'mid the forest green.   For thee the streams
Were weed-crowned Gods, with voices sweet and low.
All Fancy's numberless creations fair
Repeopled nature; for at last, at last,
The long-lost world of Hellas had been found;
The Sea of Ages, in whose silent depths
Antiquity lay buried, then cast up
Its richest treasures.   Every passing day
Brought some new waif: a priceless manuscript,
A noble statue, or an antique gem.
Italian painters did what once the Greeks
Had done in marble, and created forms
Of lasting beauty.   Nay, the very Gods
Of Greece revived, and on the canvas stood
Disguised as saints.   On capital and frieze
The curly Greek Acanthus bloomed again

[1] Pius II., Enea Silvio dei Piccolomini, 1405-1464.
[2] Part of Lorenzo de Medici's poem of " Ambra " will be found among the translations at the end of this volume.

Beneath the chisel; Tritons spouted high
From Tuscan founts; and Greek divinities
Peeped from the oaken carvings of a chair.
Those days are far; though still the Sea of Time
Casts on the shore, at intervals, a waif—
An armless Venus or a shattered Faun—
From the great wreck of Greek antiquity.
And who can tell what treasures of the past
Still in the bosom of the future lie?
All sleeping beauty must at last awake,
Nor in its sleep grows old.

        But I perceive
That, in my flight through ages, I have left
The Dwarf behind me, somewhere in the tenth
Or the eleventh century, his own
Black times. He suits these better days but ill ;
So let him in his own black times remain.

THE LADDER.

LIFE is a ladder which we all must climb;
Some climb alone and some in company;
Some clad in purple, some in tattered rags:
Some climb it followed by their fellow-men
In livery, and some by hungry duns;
Some followed by policemen half the way;
Some climb the ladder boldly, sword in hand,
And others slowly, yawning at each step;
And each man bears a load upon his back:
With one it is a heavy bag of gold;
Another upwards with a load of aches,
Or, worse, a load of evil conscience goes,
All with a weight of care. And all along
The ladder's length are overhanging boughs,
With fruits and flowers for the strong to pluck;
But many, snatching, overreach and fall.
And there are boughs, beneath whose grateful shade
We fain would stop, but we are hurried on,
As in a treadmill, to the journey's end;
And woe to him who looks too far ahead,
Nor feels each step that comes beneath his foot.
Much angry hustling on the way occurs;

The steps are narrow, and the crowd is great :
Some men, in mounting, cling to others' skirts,
But some to others lend a helping hand,
And care but little how they fare themselves.
Some on the ladder write their names for those
Behind to read, but most can leave no trace.
Most climbers drop before they get half-way ;
Some, jostled off by treacherous neighbours, fall ;
And some jump off, of their own sad accord.
But few are those who reach the topmost bars,
With hair fast whitening as they upward go,
And gathering honours as they take each step ;
And when once there, they heave a gentle sigh,
And, scarcely conscious, softly smile—and die.

THE WARNING.

I stood with others in a Paris street,
And watched the soldiers marching to the war.
Their silken colours fluttered in the breeze,
Their polished bayonets glittered in the sun,
Their martial music played a merry tune,
And each man bore a flower or sprig of green
Stuck in his cap, or fastened to his gun;
And as they went, they loudly laughed and sang,
And aimed a jest at many a looker-on.
But all around a gloomy silence reigned,
And not a word in answer did they get,
But every face a look of pity wore.
'Tis strange, I thought, that those who die should laugh,
And those should mourn whose fate it is to live.
An old old woman standing by my side,
All shrunk and bent, with hair as white as snow,
Put out her hands and cried aloud, "O God!
The wretched boys are singing! Don't they know
That they are marching to the butcher's shop?"
But all unheeding passed the human stream;
Her warning words fell on no ear but mine.
She still stood there long after they had passed,

And still I saw her shake her aged head,
As the gay sounds in distance died away.
And well she might; ere three short weeks had passed,
Most of those men were killed at Mars-la-Tour.
'Tis thus perhaps the white-winged angels stand
By the roadside of this our daily life,
And wring their hands, and call in vain to stop,
As we pass by, with jest and laugh and song,
And hurry on to many a bitter end.
Man laughs the loudest on the road to ruin—
A hollow laugh, no doubt, but loud enough
To drown the voice that warns him of his fate.

THE STORY OF A TRUNK.

A SIMPLE tale about a common thing—
Or rather say, it is no tale at all,
But a mere sketch.   But oft prosaic things
Possess a deeper pathos for the heart,
When on them falls a tear of pity shed
At hope deferred or petty tyranny,
Than all the lyrics born of laurelled brows.
A poor French governess had, in ten years
Of patient work in Russia, earned enough
To found a schoolroom in her native land.
As evil fate would have it, she returned
Just at the moment when the war broke out
Between the French and Germans.   Who forgets
Those July days of fatal 'Seventy,
All dark and sultry with the coming storm ;
When, like an omen, all the Paris leaves
Came prematurely whirling to the ground :
When on both sides was hurried mustering
Of horse and foot ; when wild confusion seized
All those who by their honest commerce lived,
And traffic ceased between the hostile States ?
She made her way to Paris, but, alas !

Her trunk remained in German hands at Köln.
Now this unlucky trunk contained wellnigh
Her little all, and, what she valued most,
Her Russian testimonials, without which
She could do nothing; and, who knows, perhaps
Some tender tokens or some letters dear,
For who can pass the earliest bloom of youth
And not have such? The poor woman wrote
And wrote again, and almost gave up hope;
But yet at last the long-wished answer came
From the officials of the rail at Köln.
All full of hope, without a moment lost,
She brought the letter for me to translate,
As she could not read German, and I could.
She might be thirty-two or thirty-three;
She was not handsome, yet I oft have seen
A handsome woman that has pleased me less,
For there was something in her eyes that said
She was not of the vulgar or the vain.
The note began with mock civility:
The writer was a soldier, and would bring
Her trunk himself to Paris very soon,
For he was going thither with his king
And full five hundred thousand German hearts,
And then. . . . I crushed the letter in my hand,
And begged that she would let me tear it up,
Because, I said, I could not read the rest,
As it contained an insult foul and base.
She nodded slowly in assent, and heaved
A sigh that seemed to say, "Can such men be?"
But spoke no word of anger nor of scorn:
For like an arrow aimed against a rock,
A jest aimed at the breast of Purity,

With blunted point falls harmless to the ground ;
And if a tear was trickling down her cheek,
I think it was not at the cruel joke,
But for her luckless trunk.   She thanked me then,
And went her way ; nor have I seen her since.
She sank in that great whirlpool of a siege.
The Prussian soldier doubtless kept his word,
And came to Paris with his regiment.
I wish that I could add that there he met
The fate that should such cowards overtake.
But 'tis more like the ways of life to think
That he returned to Prussia, with his share
Of laurels and a medal on his breast,
While the poor victim of his insolence
Stood hours daily in the melting snow,
To get her share of black and mouldy bread ;
As many a thousand other women did,
With no reward, except a smile from heaven.

THE STARER.

I CALL to mind a little silent scene
I one day witnessed in a quiet street.
The war had barely hurried to its close;
The dead were buried, and the wounded men
Were slowly now emerging from their beds,
And feebly crawling in the April sun—
Pale, broken shadows of their former selves.
An open carriage stood before a door,
And on a chair had just been lifted in
A young lieutenant of the French Hussars,
Crippled for life by fragments of a shell.
As his attendant left him for a while,
To seek for something left within the house,
A woman of the lower classes, plain,
Shabbily dressed and elderly, took up
Her stand close to the carriage door, and stared.
She stared in so intent and strange a way.
No human creature could have stood it long.
The wounded youth in turn looked hard at her.
And on his brow a gathering frown appeared.
That plainly said, "Now, woman, pass thy way.
For thou hast stared enough at me."   When lo!

B

A sudden change came o'er his pallid face,
And like a cloud the frown from off it passed;
A something in the woman's eye had gleamed,
A murmured word had dropped upon his ear,
That showed she stared in pity at his woe,
And not in mere offensive idleness.
The wounded youth stretched out a feeble arm,
And gently pressed the woman's hand in his;
And then the carriage bore him swift away.
A stare is ever an unseemly thing;
But still I think that such a stare as this,
If humbly pleaded at the gate of heaven,
By some excluded Peri of to-day,
Would gain admittance for that erring soul.

SUNSET SKETCHES.

I.

IN THE PLAIN OF LOMBARDY.

'Tis sweet in early summer, at the close
Of a long dreamy afternoon, to stand
Upon the lower slope of Apennine,
Above Æmilia's capital, and look
On to the plain of northern Italy.
Below is stretched the many-towered town,
A world of brown tile roofs, from which, confused,
A hum of life uprises and a sound
Of many bells; the boundless plain, which is
At first a maze of gardens, villas, walls,
Of fields of corn and hemp crossed and recrossed
By lanes of green acacia and of elm,
Becomes a bluish Lombardy immense,
With here and there a whitish patch which may
Be Modena or Reggio, or aught else.
And so it keeps until the set of sun,
When, letting fancy play, we might suppose
That the great Painter of the Universe
Displays his palette to the eyes of all ;
A skyey palette, on whose western edge
Are spread, at random, all the brilliant hues

Requiréd for the morrow's work ; required
To paint the fruits and flowers of the world,
The fields, the meads, the woods, the lakes, the hills,
And the broad ocean.   There are long bright streaks
Of crimson on a golden ground, and green
And crocus, saffron, orange, pearl, and tints
Purpureal, fitted for some brighter world
Than this of ours ; and through the whole there shines
A wondrous light, transcendent, which divides
In fan-like rays.   But it is well to turn
Away before the earth and sky relapse
Into the tintless twilight, and the hour
Brings something like a sadness to the heart.

II.

ON THE ALPS.

Say, have ye stood at eve in Chamonix,
And watched the boundless slopes of snow and ice
That midway hang between the earth and heaven,
Lit up and bathed with crimson by the sun,
When to itself the mountain seems to take
All that there is of colour in the world?
Then, when the transient flush has reached its height,
And for a moment in its glory stood,
It quickly fades into a paler pink,
Which next becomes a dove colour that wanes
Into a grey.   And then the chill of death
Appears to pass upon the giant mass
That cold and dull and unsubstantial stands,
And mingles in the twilight with the sky.

THE MOON-FIEND.

It is the forest in the dead of night,
Moonlit and beautiful. The silence weighs
Oppressive on the mind; and fancies come
Unbidden, for the old and moss-grown trees
Take shapes most human, and they seem to watch
The lonely traveller, lest he should chance
To overhear the secrets which they pass
Unto each other. See, their leafy heads
Incline and touch, and then the whisper runs
From tree to tree.
                    A single rider goes
Across the forest through the night; and now
The road lies by interminable pools
Of sleeping water left by recent floods.
Far as the eye can see on either hand
Is moonlit water and the trunks of trees
Mossy and ancient; overhead the boughs.
The forest in its sleeping beauty seems
Implanted in a pure and moonlit lake,
Through which the horse and rider thread their way.
The trembling column which the moon projects
Upon the water, dances by their side,

Playing at hide-and-seek behind the trees.
Why starts the horse thus with a sudden fear,
And trembling, with distended nostrils, stands,
Rooted to earth?   Why does the rider feel
A sudden thrill strike strangely through his frame?
Upon the water, there among the trees,
Now seen, now hidden, moves a female form,
Bathed in the moonlight, in a silvery dress,
Which mingles with the water as she glides,
And dies away in a long rippling wake.
No words she utters as she moves along:
But when she seems about to disappear
Behind the trees, she slowly turns and shows
Her deadly beauty to the traveller,
And beckons twice.   And on the following morn
They find him lying in the road, beside
The stagnant pool; and near him stands his horse,
And wistful looks, and neighs as if for help.

A SUMMER STORM.

A sigh seems by awakening Nature heaved—
A sigh that passes on from tree to tree,
And misses not a single blade of grass
In yonder fields. The greyish olive-trees
Turn white as if by magic, and appear
Endowed with life. The aspens by the stream
Become a silver ripple, and the stream
Itself is backward brushed by hand unseen
And rapid; while the few dead leaves upon
The road are suddenly caught up
And whirl. And then a sound which is this time
Not Nature's sigh, but Nature's hiss, runs through
The valley, and the tallest trees are bent
Like wands. Then, Earth, thy chastisement begins.
And angry Heaven's cruel lash of rain
Falls on thy hilly shoulders. To the storm
All quickly yields: the light-green rising corn
Is beaten down and lies in clotted sheaves:
The vines which lately were in garlands hung
Between the poplars, are torn off, and stream
High in the wind. But a few moments more,

And all is over.   The rain is falling still,
But there is calm; and men can look abroad,
And through the rain see sunlight on the hills.
No sound is heard around, save the dull roar
Of the augmented stream, until the note
Of some impatient bird strikes on the ear,
From dripping boughs.

THE TWINS.

Know ye the fate of that unhappy Twin
Who, to his brother bound by fleshy tie
Unseverable, woke one day to find
That brother dead, and felt himself alive ?
And how, in frightful company with Death,
He died, of an unutterable fear ?

There be two other twins of ancient race,
Body and Mind, bound by like fatal tie;
Ordained to walk through life with equal step,
And under pain most horrible condemned
To leave the world together, even as
They entered it.   Woe to the longer-lived !
Woe to the Body when the mind has fled,
Poor helpless clod, that knows not where to turn !
But worse the fate of the imperious Mind,
Born to create, to soar, and to command,
That wakes one day and finds its brother dead,
And calls upon him vainly to arise ;
Bound to a corpse, it feels the thrill of life.

POMPEII.

No trace remained upon the face of earth
Of those forgotten cities which lay deep
Entombed, in all their beauty, at the foot
Of treacherous Vesuvius, but whose fate
Had once appalled mankind.   The world was old:
Near twice a thousand springs had passed since then,
Near twice a thousand autumns.   Year by year
The unsuspecting peasant drove his plough
Above the sleeping streets, and year by year
The rustling ripple of the golden corn
Passed and repassed with every shifting breeze;
While underneath, until the day should come,
The fresco and mosaic still endured
In all the freshness of their pristine tints,
And all the records of a daily life,
So like our own, brought to a sudden stop,
As by a day of judgment premature
And partial, lay intact.   And now we stroll
In these unburied streets, or sit and watch
The bright green panting lizards as they dart
And pause, and peep, and dart again among
The antique walls and pavements; while the mind

Gets ever nearer to Antiquity,
Until the great catastrophe appears
In all its vivid horror.   Once again
The city lives, nor fears.   We see its throng,
Its sunny beauty and its carelessness,
The many coloured awnings of its streets,
Its verdure, and its flowers, and its fruits,
Its houses, and their shady inner courts;
We even hear the splash of fountains still.
When dreamy noontide's heat had lulled the mind,
And Nature basked in sunshine; when the capes
And distant hills were shadowy and faint;
When all was listless, and no sound was heard
Save lapping wavelets of the tideless sea;
When every flower drooped its languid head,
And air was heavy with the August scents,
Day turned to night; the face of earth was changed,
And Hell let loose on Heaven;—for what shores
Could claim the name of Heaven, if not these ?
In that unnatural gloom none knew or cared
When came the real night, which brought no peace;
But ever and anon, with lurid glare,
The torches of the fugitives, who sought
Each other in the quickly altering streets,
Lit up the falling ashes, and exposed
Some face of horror.   High above the shouts—
Above the unknown sounds that came from earth—
Above the crash of columns and of walls,—
Rose the shrill cry of wounded animals,
Or shriek of women trodden under foot.
Death came from every side.   The wretches found
No safety in the courage of despair,
No pity in the elements.   The air

Was heavy with the ever-falling ash,
Like lurid snowdrifts in the plains of Hell;
The waving earth refused to bear their steps,
Or suddenly enwrapt them in their flight
With vapours deadly and invisible, which made
The mother drop the babe she held, the bride
Her bridegroom's hand, the miser drop his gold
And bite the dust; and then the ashes hid
Their bodies; while, in cellars too secure,
Where many sought for life, Death took his time,
And dealt in nameless horrors, as with him
Who, taking refuge with his dog, died first,
And then was eaten.   But all this was deep
Beneath the livid ashes which enclosed
Pompeii now, and hid her from the world.

II.

ELEGIES

A CHRISTMAS ELEGY.

GENTLE, with ours compared, is the rudest of Italy's winters :
  Ever at hand is the sun, ready all ills to repair;
Green are the garments of earth, and almost as fresh as in summer;
  Warm are the tints of the hills, free are the rivers from ice.
There amid holm-oaks and bays, and laurels and trellises verdant,
  Winter, while Spring is asleep, stealeth his flowery garb;
Ay, and his heavenly smile; so that those with Winter familiar,
  Meeting him thus in disguise, hail him, delighted, as Spring.
Yet, notwithstanding this beauty, that Italy wears in the winter,
  Almost a prison it seems, when I remember the North.
Where, in his mantle of snow, with icicles bearded and hoar-frost,
  Winter holds Nature for months, clasped in his shaggy embrace.
For, in the lands that are cold, there resideth a poetry homely,
  Cosiness-loving and sweet, ne'er understood in the South.
Born of the long winter evenings, it lurks by the hearth that is cheery,
  When, in the darkness outside, moaneth the pitiless wind :
Living in customs ancestral, with rough hospitality mingled,
  Unto the homes of the North great is the charm that it lends.
There was my boyhood spent, and memories dear of Christmas
  Often come home to my mind out of the years that are dead :
Fir-trees all covered with toys, and blazing with numberless tapers,
  Filling the room with a scent, mingled of fir and of wax—

Pyramids radiant and rich : and the faces of children around them,
  Happy and wistful and sweet, waiting with wonder their share ;
Puddings encircled with flame, and pies for the Gods too delicious ;
  Customs derived from the past, cheering both body and soul ;
Branches of holly all prickly, with beautiful berries of scarlet ;
  Branches of mistletoe strange, laden with berries of white.
Outdoor memories too : the feel of the snow in its crispness,
  Taking the print of the foot, softly, with faintest of creaks ;
Or, where the snow has been swept, the ring of the earth that is frozen
  Under the foot as you stamp, warming the limbs that are numb ;
Snow from the branches dislodged, by the breeze that is gentle and fitful,
  Falling in spray to the ground, bright in the sun without heat ;
Snowballing furious and fast, and the thud of the well-patted snow-
        ball,
  Stopped by a wall or a tree, leaving its record behind ;
Dead leaves white with the frost, and bushes with crystals incrusted.
  Sparkling and delicate fur, turning to silver the twigs.
Still insecure is the ice ; and the boys are hovering round it,
  Cautiously trying its strength, keeping one foot on the brink,
Throwing a stone now and then, that sings as it bounds o'er its surface :
  Only the boldest advance, braving the ominous cracks.
Skaters begin to appear, the sky with anxiety watching ;
  Strong enough soon is the ice ; soon is the fun at its height.
Slides by the margin are formed ; the sliders press close on each other.
  Shouting with glee as they go, falling at last in a heap.
Booths on the banks are erected, by vendors of comforting liquors.
  Or by the letters of skates : idlers by dozens arrive,
Watching the crowd of the skaters revolving in circles incessant,
  Flitting like shadows unheard, swiftly in maze without end ;
Poised on the breadth of a hair, and moving in beautiful balance.
  Backwards or forwards at will, over the surface new born.
Mighty enchanter was he, who, taking advantage of Nature's
  Temper most transient, the frost, furnished this art unto men ;

Teaching them motions unknown, and which seemed out of reach of
    their species ;
  Choosing, as field of his skill, that which is gone in a day !
Beautiful art that I loved, by a cruel denial of movement
    Rendered still dearer now, ne'er shall I know thee again.
Lost are these pastimes for me, with the North I shall never return to—
    Lost with the health that is gone—lost with the years that have fled.
Only their memories last ; the reality long has departed,
    Even as vanished the ice, touched by the breath of the thaw.

OXFORD.

Fast is the pace that we go, in the first of the stages successive,
  After the journey of life once has been fairly begun.
Seldom we stop to look back, and to measure the distance accomplished;
  If we should happen to turn, 'tis for a moment, not more.
Only when time has elapsed, and the climbing grows ever more rugged,
  Fairly we stop and look back, searching the plain underneath.
Cities and houses we see, through which we have passed on the journey,
  Leaving in each as we went that which we cannot reclaim.
Ten are the years that are past; and now, on the arduous pathway,
  Sadly I turn and look round, searching in memory's plain.
Many the cities I see, but one above all in its beauty,
  Slowly, as rises the mist, taketh a tangible shape.
Colleges many and old, that nestle 'mid foliage ancestral,
  Near to a river I see, covered with lightest of craft;
Pleasant and pensive retreats, whose beautiful inner quadrangles
  Look upon carpets of turf, fit for the feet of a queen.
Blackened and battered by time is the stone that for ever is crumbling,
  Yet has for centuries stood, yet may for centuries stand.
Beautiful precincts medieval, connected with all that is greatest,
  Softened and hallowed by age, peopled for ever by youth!
Many are we who look back, with mingled affection and sadness,
  Unto the days that we spent, happy and young, in your shade.

Fairer and dearer ye grow, as the number of summers and winters
  Slowly augments unperceived, since we have bidden adieu.
Fairer and dearer ye grow, as we feel how since then we have altered;
  If we returned for a day, scarce would ye know us again.
He whom ye knew as so gay, has become an habitual grumbler,
  Not having met in the world that which he thought was his due.
He who was open of heart, has grown to be cold and suspicious;
  He who the wittiest was, dull has become from routine.
Even the man that succeeds, and is working his way to the woolsack,
  Or to a surplice of lawn, or to the Ministers' bench,
Thinks with a sigh of regret of the time of his youth by the Isis,
  Caring the less for the prize as it approaches his grasp.
All of us something have lost, that we know we can never recover,
  Graver we go our ways, bearing our burden of care.
Oxford I fondly remember: the hall in its noble proportions,
  Panelled with blackest of oak, old as the college itself;
Where are arrayed all around the portraits of dead benefactors,
  Wearing their garb of the past—faces severe and sedate,
Which by the tremulous flare of the giant fireplace lighted,
  Restless appear in their frames, taking the queerest of shapes.
Under them tables are ranged, where the clatter of tongues and of
    tankards,
  Mixed with the noisy jest, tells of the presence of youth.
All, save the table supreme, where the Dons in their glory are sitting,
  High out of reach of the crowd, raised on a platform of state.
Yes, and the chapel I see, to which in the mornings we hurried;
  Round it, in cap and in gown, gathers a numerous group.
Near to the door, in a niche, a figure in stone of the Virgin,
  Headless and mouldering, stands, telling of Catholic days.
Likewise of oak is the chapel, with windows whose tinted reflections,
  Orange and purple and green, fall on the pavement of stone.
Still I the chapel-bell hear, and a sound, as of choristers, cometh
  Fainter but beautiful still, back through the distance of years.

Pretty and snug were my rooms; they looked on the Common Room
    Building;
Under the windows, the lawn stretched in its ample extent.
Could I revisit the place, I think I should hesitate somewhat
    Ere I set foot in them now, different from what they were then.
Unto the room he is fond of, the occupant quickly imparteth
    Something we cannot define,—part, as it were, of himself—
Maybe it lies in the way that the inmate his furniture places;
    Maybe it lies in the things carelessly scattered about.
'Tis the most transient of gifts, which, different in mind, his successor,
    Scarce has he entered the room, ruthlessly brushes away.
Who in my rooms is installed? the thought has its charm and its
    sadness;
Nothing but this can I tell—different he is from myself.
Is it a rowing-man strong, whose existence is all in his muscles,
    Sitting there tired, inert, after the work of the day?
What if a reading man 'tis, whose "oak" is unceasingly "sported,"
    Sitting alone with his lamp, working till daylight shall dawn?
What if a dreamer it is, or religious enthusiast ardent,
    Left to himself by the rest, brooding o'er life and its aims?
Or is the occupant fast, and never alone for a moment;
    Lavish of breakfasts and "wines," constantly playing at cards?
Strong is the scent of cigars, the scout on the staircase is ever
    Cider-cup fetching in haste, or sherry-cobbler and straws.
Oh, how the life of those days recurs as I write, and is vivid!
    Faces of old college friends, details forgotten return.
Oxford, not perfect art thou; but let not thy faults be remembered;
    Here, where in sadness I write, asking for nought but a sigh!
Only the things that are good, and memories dear to many,
    Let me attempt to recall, leaving forgotten all else.
Wholesome are Latin and Greek, but the best of the lessons that
    Oxford
    Unto her children imparts, not in the schools must be sought;

Many indeed are their forms, derived from the spirit that dwelleth
    Lastingly over the place, born of tradition and time.
Good is the residence here, in these colleges ancient, poetic ;
    Here, if it ever was true, sermons are written in stones.
Good is the intercourse free with minds that are active and varied,
    Favouring all that is best, courtesy, manliness, thought.
Good are the long-drawn debates, where eloquence, destined to conquer,
    Measures its pinions, and youth borrows the wisdom of age.
Good are the walks in the country, through hamlets with ivy-clad
    churches ;
    Whiling, in talk with one's chum, gently the hours away.
Yes, and the long afternoons that with him one spends on the river,
    Lazily mooring the skiff under the boughs that o'erhang.
What has become of thee, Grahame, since letters, grown rarer and
    rarer,
    Ceased altogether, and Fate led us so widely apart ?
Many a morsel, since then, of the bitterest bread have I eaten ;
    Wiser thou wast than myself, happier I hope thou hast been !
Good are the pastimes athletic, and good is the heart-stirring boat-race.
    Nobly contested and won, fairest of sights in the world.
Say, have you stood on the bank, when the Eights, after leaving the
    barges,
    Swiftly yet leisurely pass, seeking their place for the start ?
Say, have you noted the oars all splendidly striking in cadence,
    Then the long feathering sweep, kissing the face of the stream ?
Match me, ye lands, if ye can, the men in their light silken jerseys,
    Flower of youth and of strength, shirking nor toil nor pain !
Heard ye the gun ? They are off ! and the hum and the flutter
    increases,
    Showing how keenly the crowd watches the fate of the race.
See, in the distance they come, and their partisans, heated and
    breathless,
    Following close on the bank, shouting for ever, Well rowed !

Look, our boat is astern; and the distance, by Jove, is decreasing!
    Louder the shouting becomes; now it has turned to a roar.
See, we are gaining upon them! the oars, as they pass through the
    water,
    Bend like a wand. It is grand! Wilder their rowing has grown.
Now for the final spurt! Well rowed! Drive it out of the water!
    Now our bow to their stern! well steered! and, by heavens, they're
    bumped!
Ah! it is long, long ago, since I shouted like this with the others;
    Many a boat has been bumped, there on that river since then.
New generations of rowers, and new generations of shouters,
    Closely each other succeed; who has a thought for the old?

ELIZABETH.

I.

DURING the weary months, when Paris, all closely surrounded,
　Fought with starvation within, fought with the Germans without ;
When, though the master of millions, no man could leave or re-enter,
　Were the need ever so great, either for others or self ;
When many knew that a word, if into the city transmitted,
　Ruin would surely avert, fatal delusion remove :
Greater perhaps was the suffering, deeper perhaps was the heart-ache,
　Caused by the stoppage of news, than by the stoppage of bread.
Those who were pining for bread were only the hapless Parisians,
　Those who were pining for news numbered both them and the world.
History, when wilt thou tell, how many the mothers too tender,
　Who in that endless suspense died for the want of a word ?
Nothing, however, so tragical lies at the root of this story :
　'Tis but a straw I picked up, drifting about in the storm.
During the period of agony, when the political centre
　Wandered from Paris to Tours, wandering thence to Bordeaux,
I was attached to an Embassy, which, with other legations,
　Shared in the fortune of war, moving as Government moved.
There at Bordeaux was the capital ; there in a heap were collected
　All the official remains saved from the general wreck :
Over-worked public departments, embassies, bodies judicial,
　Newspaper offices, banks, great Paris houses of trade ;
Also a nondescript crowd of such as in time of invasion
　Hang on the footsteps of power, feeding on public disgrace :

Place-hunters, demagogues, spies, contractors, soldiers of fortune ;
    All who had nothing to lose, or who had something to gain.
Somehow 'twas rumoured abroad, the embassy could, as a favour,
    Letters to Paris transmit, over the enemy's lines,
Having been granted the privilege, by the high Prussian command-
    ers,
    Messengers thither to send bearing what letters it chose.
This was a cruel mistake, for we could no more an admittance
    Into the city obtain, than could the rest of the world.
Letters, however, and messages, all of them destined for Paris,
    At our office poured in, in a continuous stream ;
Nearly all being accompanied by a most pressing entreaty,
    Giving a view of the case, showing how great was the need.
Piteous, indeed, were the narratives, proving what suffering tortured
    During that weary siege thousands within and without;
When all the notes to be forwarded treated of matters so urgent,
    Friends and relations to save, heartrending fears to appease,
Difficult is it to justify what my attention could rivet
    On a particular note, urgent far less than the rest.
Who can dissect all the principles which our feelings determine,
    Fancy who can control, sympathy who can direct ?
I know no reason to give, except individual humour,
    What brings a smile to the one brings to the other a tear.
She who the letter had sent, by name was Elizabeth Burton,
    Writing from England, I think, much in the following terms :
" Humbly I beg of your lordship not to reject my petition,
    Merely to forward this note, which I have made very small ;
'Tis to my landlord I write, but one little line of entreaty,
    Just to take care of my room, saying that I shall return.
Ah ! how little I dreamt, when but for three days I left Paris,
    So many months would elapse ere I should see it again !
Not until now have I realised what a home Paris was for me ;
    Nor, till I saw it no more, how I that little room loved.

Carefully locking the door, I carried the key into exile ;
    There on the table it lies, useless but dear old friend.
Summer was hot when I left; the window remained all wide open ;
    Now it is bitterly cold ; snowstorm and rain must drive in.
Ah ! how the scene must be desolate, where all was lately so happy !
    Dead are the flowers I loved ; starved are the birds in the cage.
Would I were back in the capital; fain would I share its privations,—
    Sew for the soldiers all day—sit by the wounded all night.
Maybe of all that I left the landlord has taken possession
    For the arrears of rent, thinking I shall not return."
As I this letter perused, and noted the writer's entreaties,
    Sorrow indeed did I feel that she had written in vain.
Much would I gladly have sacrificed but for the means to assist her.
    Twice I the letter re-read, then put it by with the rest.
Who was Elizabeth Burton, who thus to high persons official
    Wrote in a tone of romance, and to their feelings appealed ?
Clearly the letter showed character, and a poetical nature :
    Doubtless the writer was young—new to the ways of the world.
Why did she live by herself, in one little room, unattended ?
    All in the letter proclaimed, free from all sin was her life.
Was she an artist perhaps, and studying painting or music ?
    Or a strange runaway girl, living alone and concealed ?
Poor the maiden was probably—poor in worldly possessions—
    But all the richer in mind, if my own instinct told true.
Thus did I let my thoughts carry me, till an ideal Eliz'beth
    Grew and took shape in my mind, fair as the dawning of day.
Beautiful power of Fancy ! Such are the slender materials
    Which for the poet suffice, forming the base of his dream.
Still dost thou live in my memory, fair little airy enchantress,—
    Such as I wished thee to look—such as I thought thee to be.
Sickened and fagged with my work — surrounded by minds uncon-
    genial—
    Loathing convention and forms—yearning for leisure and friends—

Oh ! in thy plain little room, how often in thought I took refuge,
  Taking my place by thy side, tending thy flowers and birds !
Say, wast thou not a reality, when from afar I beheld thee ?
  Comfort and friend of those days, say, wast thou only a dream ?

II.

Nearly a year had gone by, and Paris had fought and surrendered ;
  Those that were in had streamed out, those that were out had streamed
    in.
France was again with her capital, after their long separation,
  Proud of its useless defence, eager to soften its wounds.
'Twas but a respite from suffering for the unfortunate city ;
  Yet had the worst to be felt, still had the Commune to come.
Light-headed Daughter of Misery, born in the gutter and sewer,
  Perfect indeed was thy work, sure thy incendiary torch !
When will the stateliest palaces, lately the models of beauty,
  Now shells empty and black, rise from their ashes again ?
Shattered the trees in the Tuileries, headless the statues of marble,
  Marked by the bullets each house, close as the holes in a sieve.
Split was the frame of society down to its lowest foundation.
  Sullen and cowed were the poor ; not reassured were the rich :
Lost was the sense of stability, gone men's belief in the future.
  Everything still seemed to lurch, after the earthquake had passed.
Yet to this dreary wilderness life was not long in returning.
  Quick was the mind that creates, busy the hand that·repairs.
Scarcely the ever re-echoing deep-voiced cannon was silent,
  Industry took to her looms, Commerce reopened her shops.
Luxury, treading uneasily in the late home of starvation,
  Slily returned in disguise, where she had openly reigned.
Pleasure, quite modest at first, and shy 'mid the general mourning,
  Now, by unnoticed degrees, sought her habitual haunts.
Scattered about by the hurricane, men were still seeking each other.
  Friend was still looking for friend, nay, often father for son.

Doctors were seeking their patients, lawyers were seeking their clients,
   Anxious to know who was ruined, anxious to know who was dead.
Tradesmen were seeking their customers, teachers were seeking their
      pupils :
   Who could retie, in a day, all that the war had cut through ?
Since my return to the capital, where all was still so exciting,
   Seeing new faces each day, meeting again with old friends,
Seldom indeed did my memory turn to the fair Correspondent
   Whom I had seen in my dreams during my stay at Bordeaux.
Still, in her youth and simplicity, fair as an opening flower,
   Did she return now and then such as she there had appeared ;
And I would catch myself wondering whether I ever should meet
      her,
   Now that she doubtless was back in her beloved little room.
As I was sitting one day, engaged on official despatches,
   One of the servants came in holding a card in his hand,
Saying a lady was there who asked to see me on business :
   Brief would she be, had she said ; only a minute—no more.
Carelessly taking the card, I read, *Miss Elizabeth Burton.*
   Written in ink were the words, in the same hand as of yore.
As she those simple words wrote, but little indeed she suspected
   What an effect they would have, how many thoughts they would
      wake.
Little she guessed I should hesitate ere I the waiting-room entered,
   Hearing the beat of my heart as I the door-handle turned.
She was alone in the room, nor heard she my step as I entered ;
   But at the window she stood, watching intently the street,
Where all the opposite houses, by fire and bullets disfigured,
   Still, with a terrible truth, told of the great city fight.
There as she stood unsuspecting, graceful enough was her figure ;
   Yet, ere I looked on her face, instinct had told me the truth :
Poor ideal Elizabeth !   Youthful and beautiful being !
   Thou that my heart had conceived, thou wast a thing of the past.

This was the end of the mystery! *This* was the end of the idyl!
　Angry I felt with myself, angry—God help me!—with *her*.
How did she dare to be otherwise than as my fancy had painted?
　Or, at least, why had she come? Why had she broken the charm?
But as I looked on the dress, all shabby and worn, she was clad in,
　And on that pale and thin face, worthier feelings returned.
Might she not once have been fair, as fair as my day-dream had seen
　her,
　Ere she was faded by time, ere she was faded by want?
And my ideal Elizabeth, were she now standing before me,
　Would she not wither one day, would she not look even thus?
Softened I hope was my voice, and gentle I hope was my manner,
　As I the window approached where the poor visitor stood.
Simple and short was her narrative: she was a teacher of English,
　And had been teaching for years when the great war-storm burst
　forth.
Little she earned by her work—her pupils were all of the humblest;
　Still she had managed to live, till all was wrecked by the siege.
During the long months of idleness, all her small savings had perished;
　All she had left in her room, landlord had sold for the rent;
Sold was her small stock of books, all presents from dear old pupils;
　Sold was her small store of dress, cruelly needed, alas!
All her old pupils were gone and scattered in different directions; .
　Some in the war had been killed, some in the siege had been ruined.
Vainly for new ones she sought; who cared to take lessons in English?
　No one had leisure to learn, no one had money to spare.
Therefore she offered her services, if I required a copyist,
　Or to do any small work, so as a trifle to earn.
Poor, pale, real Elizabeth! frail withered leaf in the tempest!
　As I looked into her face, almost my dream I forgot.
Something I gave her to do; and secretly vowed to befriend her,
　Half for reality's sake, half for the sake of a myth.

THE FLUTE-PLAYER.[1]

THAT which on earth is the frailest, Time with his scythe often misses;
  Sweeping a city away, leaving unbroken a vase.
Who does not often exclaim, as he treads in the steps of the Mower.
  "Strength, indeed thou art weak; weakness, indeed thou art strong!"
Come, I will show you a tomb—'tis that of an ancient Etruscan;
  In it a woman's remains, crumbling away into dust.
See still intact is a Flute, in what was the hand of the player;
  Centuries twenty, nay more, mute has it lain by her side.
Dead is the race she belonged to, and dead is the language she uttered,
  Dead are the laws she obeyed, dead is the creed that she held;
Yet her ephemeral presence hath left us a tangible vestige;
  Empires leave but a name; that which endures is a Flute.
Doubtless her music was primitive, yet for the Gods all-sufficient,
  If it was good for her time, if in men's ears it was sweet.
Flute, be a potent enchanter, and come to the aid of my fancy;
  Clothe her again in the flesh, such as she stood in her day;
Youth to her figure restore, Beauty bestow on her features;
  Some of the breath that she gave, give to the player again.
Shape hath she taken already. How strangely distinct is the phantom!
  Fairer, perhaps, than in life; fiction is fairer than truth.

[1] Written after a visit to the Etruscan Museum at Bologna.

Even the music I hear; 'tis faint, and as if from a distance;
   Simple and plaintive the air, young is the musical art.
Why does she stop in her playing, and listless, the instrument holding,
   Wistfully gaze into space, lost in the mazes of thought?
Tell me thy story, O maiden! all language is clear to the poet,
   When it in purity comes straight from the depths of the heart.
See, on the lips of the player a word of emotion is trembling. . . .
   Ah! I awake from my dream—all, save the flute, melts to air.

A BLIND BEGGAR.

Hard is the fate of the blind, the blind that are rich and are read to:
  What of the fate of the poor, plunged in a night without end?
Woe to the blind without friends, or whose friends are illiterate rustics!
  Blindness for them is a grave, worse than the grave that will come.
In it the mind is enclosed, and decays, in its dark isolation,
  Slowly, as years pass away, bringing nor help nor relief.
Now I will draw you a picture, and almost still life I may call it:
  Merely a beggar who sits near to the door of a church;
There in the morning they place him, and thence in the evening they
    take him,
  Nought does he hear but the steps, hastening by in the streets;
Early 'tis yet in the morning; he leans on the base of a pillar;
  Turned to the sky is his face; open his eyes that are dead.
Scarce has he reached middle age; and he bears that expression of
    patience,
  Which to the features of man blindness alone can impart.
Yes, it is early as yet, the children to school are proceeding;
  Some, as the beggar they pass, twitch at his hair or his beard.
Slowly the hours pass by; and only at intervals lengthy
  Slightly his body he shifts, easing his stiffening limbs.
What doth the mind in its prison, as slowly the sun in the heavens
  Rises and reaches the noon, shedding no light for this man?

Does he the past reconstruct, and dwell on the days that were happy,
　When of the banquet of life still he could humbly partake?
Or on the days of suspense, when fast he was losing his eyesight,
　Ere he had sunk into calm, ere resignation had come?
Hard did he struggle and fight, to see through the film that was
　thick'ning
Cruelly, day by day, closing him in by degrees;
Straining with sickening heart to give to the vapoury outlines,
　Shapes more precise and exact; vaguer and vaguer they grew.
All things to shadows had turned, and the shadows grew fainter and
　fainter,
　Till in the gloom they were lost,—twilight had passed into night.
Poor ill-fated mechanic! Think'st thou that thou art the first one
　Who against Nature has fought, when she retakes what she gave?
Low is the sun in its course, and long are already the shadows,
　Still he is there and unchanged, turned is his face to the sky;
Less a man does he seem, than a plant of a form that is human,
　Asking no friendship or care, needing no converse on earth;
Almost he seems to be dead; but once or twice, when a copper
　Into his hand has been dropt, low has he murmured his thanks.
Cold is the breeze of the evening; his face and his fingers are whiter;
　No other change does he show, since he was placed there at morn.
Now it is twilight at last; the children from school are returning;
　Some, as the beggar they pass, pull him again by the hair;
Many the steps that he hears, and quick do they fall on the pavement:
　All are in haste to get home, after the work of the day.
Few cast a glance as they hasten; but some as they pass by this
　beggar,
　Seeing him motionless still, wish they could think that he sleeps.

AN APRIL ELEGY.

SEEK for no omens in spring: the face of the spring is deceptive;
　Ask not the leaves that are new ever a hope to confirm;
No, nor put faith in the birds renewing their chorus of promise;
　Old is the song that they sing, old as the world and deceit.
Ye who seek omens in spring, have ye ne'er, in the course of existence,
　Noted the fate that on earth follows the things that are fair?
Sadness there lurks in the air, in the air that is balmy, of April,
　Even as under a smile, often a boding is hid.
Vague is the feeling and dreamy; a sense of the ill that the future
　Bringeth to what is too fair, bringeth to what is too good.
Ah, I remember a day, when the blossoms, as now, in the orchards,
　Lay in a heap as in flakes, close round the stem of each tree;
When, in the air of the morning, a shower had left, as at present,
　Odours earthy and rare, when it was sweet to be out;
When, as in love with herself, and oblivious of all that is fleeting,
　Nature, restored unto youth, smiled in her beauty divine:
All that is freshest and sweetest, she laid on her board in profusion,
　Freely their share of her feast bidding all beings to take.
All that had, torpid for months, reposed on the bosom of winter,
　Bursting the numbing embrace, stepped into life at her call;
All that was injured and ill, obeying the quickening summons,
　Crawled in the warmth of the sun, feeling a moment of strength.
Thus, among others, a youth, at last on this morning of mornings,
　After long weary months spent in seclusion and pain,
Feeble and dizzy, emerged, and looked on the earth in her beauty,
　Just at the moment when spring wholly her garb had renewed.

D

All was so new and so strange; the trees and the houses familiar,
  Different from what they had been, larger or smaller, appeared.
Yet, when a moment had passed, and things had resumed their
  proportions,
Nought in the landscape was changed; only the season was new.
Taking the hand of the friend who had watched by his bed in his
  illness,
Sadly and faintly the youth murmured this final appeal:
" Look how the leaves are unfurled ! how the blossoms are strewn on
  the pathway !
List to the song of the birds, there in the boughs overhead !
Ah, what a beautiful world ! no, never so fair have I seen it;
  Why is it shown to me thus, if I so soon must depart ?
Is there, ye leaves, of the life that is poured at this time without
  measure
Into the lap of the world, no tiny portion for me ?
Not when all Nature revives, and the sunshine of April all-healing,
  Raises the flower that droops, nipped by the frost of the night ?
Not when all creatures that be, on earth and in air and in water,
  Quiver with strength new-infused ? Am I alone left behind ?
Am I forgotten by spring ? " But Nature smiled on in her beauty,
  Listening not to his prayer, breathed at her opening feast.
All on his footpath was transient; the things he invoked were all
  fleeting ;
Scarce had they come into life, all disappeared from the scene.
Where was the green overhead, and the birds with their singing that
  filled it ?
Where was the green under foot, six little months from that day ?
This was the last of his springs ; and the first of the vapours autumnal,
  Ended his poor reprieve, ended his hope and his fear.
None should too rashly found hopes on the sunshine of April; for
  autumn,
Silent and pallid and bare, treads in the footsteps of spring.

VENICE.

Time is the greatest of painters; he adds to the fabrics of genius
   That which no genius on earth ever has learned to impart.
Tints on his palette are spread, which the artist will never discover;
   All that is harsh he subdues, making harmonious the whole.
Slowly he works, and unseen; and, alas! as he painteth he weakens;
   Beauty he gives with his right, strength he removes with his left.
This is the price of his work; but art, though it be of the highest,
   If at perfection it aims, needeth his finishing touch.
Where has he worked as at Venice, this hoary old painter primeval?
   Where, with more generous hand, lavished his beautiful tints?
Look at the stately canal, a witness of pageants forgotten,
   Which, like a serpent immense, winds through the city of isles.
There do the palaces stand, whose names are familiar from story—
   Names that might long be deceased, had not the poet been there.
Proud in their cruel desertion, they ask not the stranger's compassion,
   Yet, as he glides through their midst, who would refuse them a sigh?
There are they ranged on the shore, in their beautiful drapery time-
     stained,
   Sadly, to all who will list, telling a tale of their youth;
Poor decrepit remains, that mournfully gaze on the waters,
   Which, like a mirror of truth, shows them how old they have grown.
There in the silent canal, the splash of the oar hath its sadness;
   He that hath heard it and sighed, knows what an elegy means.

Venice, how clearly I see thee : the palace massive and splendid,
    Where, in the days of the past, thou didst thy Doges enthrone ;
Where, in the great inner court, the sinister tablets of marble
    Tell us the name of the wretch, there to the waters condemned ;
Where, in the eloquent gloom, the air is with mystery laden,
    All that is dead rising up ; ay, and the square of St Mark,
Where the basilica stands, with its many round cupolas zinc-clad,
    Calling the thoughts to the East, back to the Byzantine days ;
Where, to a measureless height, the massive quadrangular belfry
    Rises, alone and sublime, into the blue of the sky ;
Where, from the ledges around, the cloud of slate-coloured pigeons,
    Daily, obedient to man, rustling, alight to be fed.
Ay, and the alleys from isle unto isle, and the numberless bridges,
    Where, as you pass on your way, gondolas shoot underneath.
Who can those bridges forget, or the miniature square in each islet,
    Where a well, fashioned of bronze, quaintly the centre adorns ?
Hard would it be to decide, in this noiseless city of islets,
    Which has more charm for the mind, whether the land or the
        deep.
Blue is the sea in the open, green in the narrower waters,
    Green and with streakings of brown under the high palace walls.
Here in the narrow canals, in the shadow of bridge and of buttress,
    All that Romance has conceived presses confused on the mind.
Time has returned on his steps, and we stand in a century by-gone ;
    All that surrounds us is great ; Venice is Venice again.
Swiftly the gondola glides in the shade and the favouring twilight,
    Rearing its rostrum of steel, curved like the neck of a swan.
Masked by its colour funereal, silent it speeds and mysterious,
    Saving the sound of the oar striking in cadence the wave.
Holding concealed in its bosom a soul that unnoted is noting.
    Is it an errand of crime ?   Is it an errand of love ?
Venice, the star of the sea, has satellites many and radiant
    Set in the placid lagoon, blue as the vault of the sky,

Motionless satellites they: the girdle of islands around her,
    Rearing their towers aloft, proud of belonging to *her*.
Grand are these towers by day, but grander by night we beheld them,
    Once when o'er city and isles hurried the Spirit of Storm.
Dost thou remember it still? How we stood at the wide-open window,
    Into the dark looking out, hearing a drop or two fall?
Then how at intervals rapid the isle of St George, by the lightning
    Stricken from out of the night, quivering came into view,
Tinged by a roseate light, and its convent and belfry stupendous
    Printed one instant the sky, vivid, more vivid than day?
Dost thou remember it still, and the ships in the harbour at anchor?
    Few in number, alas! silent are now the lagoons—
Emptiness here, but not ruin. Venice still stands in her glory,
    Such as she stood in her day when she was Queen of the seas,
Seeming, as years pass away, to utter a piteous entreaty:
    Greatness, Prosperity, come! all as ye left it remains;
Empty but splendid is all: the shell of a greatness departed;
    Sad is the splendour intact, sadder than many a ruin.
Gone is the soul of the place; but the body in beauty endureth,
    Fair as the eye can behold, more so perhaps than in life.
Death has a beauty at times, that entrances the poet and painter:
    Pale though she be and inert, Venice in death hath a smile;
Lying in state as it were, with her crown of towers eternal,
    Stretched on a mantle of blue, draped in her marbles of yore.
No, she was never more fair, since the day that she rose from the
    waters,
    Formed, like the Goddess of Love, out of the foam of the sea.

LAURA.

DEATH, with the noiseless step, whose form has appeared on my thresh-
old,
Turns and proceeds on his way, knocking at other men's doors ;
Ay, at the doors of the strong, at the doors of the young and the
happy,
Even of those who, of late, seemed out of reach and secure.
Death, O thou Thing inconsistent, that snatchest, in passing, the blos-
som,
Leaving the fruit that is ripe, ready to drop at thy touch,
Were there not others to take on the path thou wast silently treading ?
Why hast thou taken this girl, surely the fairest that was ?
What ! when so many there be, whose mission on earth is accom-
plished,
Waiting thy call undismayed, laden with honours and years—
What ! when so many there be, who are lying in pain and implore
thee,
Wretches to whom, from disease, life has a burden become—
What ! when so many there be, who are plucking the hem of thy gar-
ment,
Courting thy chilly embrace, sated with ills undeserved,—
This is the one thou selectest ? a creature of youth and of beauty
Still all in love with her life ?   Death, thou art wanton indeed !

ROME.

I.

Rome, are they changing thy face, and is it not such as I loved it,
  Dreamy, impressive, and grand?   Rome, are they making thee
    young?
Often I think of that winter: the rule of the Pontiffs still lasted;
  Rome was the place of the past; nought of the present she knew;
Freedom she knew not, nor science, nor many a thing that ennobles;
  Silent she lived, and inert, courting prosperity not.
But she possessed for the poet a magic, a drowsy enchantment:
  Something elegiac and rare, due to the power of Time.
Time is the staple of elegy; Time and the multiform action,
  Slow and poetic and sad, which it exerts on the world.
Rome was the city of ages, and such as the ages had made her,
  Working by gentle degrees; who could be dead to the charm?
Yet it was clear unto all, that the dyke which repelled innovation,
  Sapped from within and without, soon would give way to the wave.
Nature abhorreth stagnation, and raises the whirlwind to end it;
  All upon earth must advance, even the Rome of the Popes.

II.

Who, that has known and loved Rome, looks not back to the first of
    the winters
  Which in her limits he spent, thinking how happy it was?

Whether we **stood** on the hill that looks down on the City Eternal,
  Letting the eye, far and wide, roam o'er its numberless roofs,
High o'er whose level the ruins uprise like vessels gigantic,
  Stranded, half buried, forlorn, wrecked on the ocean of Time;
Or in the galleries strolled, 'mid the silent people of marble,
  Gifted with beauty divine—ay, and perpetual youth,
Who so placid look on, while the world grows old, and we mortals
  Pass before them and die, after a life of a day;
Whether we lingered at dusk in the churches heavy with incense,
  While, o'er the organ's deep peal, rose the high voices clear;
Or in the villas in May, among masses of bay and of ilex,
  Gathering, down in the dells, bunches of cyclamens pink;
Equally great was the charm, and beauty was ever around us;
  Give me, ye Powers of Good, give me those days that are gone!
Give me again the delight, which a mind that was youthful and ardent
  Felt, as the realms of the Past suddenly then were disclosed,
Dull and unreal no more, as they seemed in the school-books, but
    real,
  Crowded with tangible forms—column, arch, statue, and bust!
Fondly I loved to repeople those silent parts of the city
  Whence long ago life had ebbed, leaving its wrecks on the shore.
Tracts where the Goth and the Vandal seem still to be present in spirit;
  Where every stone that you pass tells the Decline and the Fall;
Where the ephemeral green and the rubbish of empire mingle;
  Where, in each desolate field, rises some landmark of Time.
Ah, they are fast disappearing, those spaces endeared to the poet:
  Workmen already are here; see, they are laying down streets.
Work, O ye masons, in peace! ye lay the first stone of a ruin:
  That which man buildeth to-day, ivy to-morrow invades.

III.

Sweet are the gardens of Rome; but one is for Englishmen sacred;
  Who, that has ever been there, knows not the beautiful spot

Where our poets are laid, in the shade of the pyramid lofty,
    Dark grey, tipped as with snow, close to the turreted walls?
Tall are the cypresses many, from which in the evenings of summer,
    Nightingale nightingale calls, soon as the twilight descends.
Nature around is profuse; the rose and the ivy are mingled;
    Fit for the poet the place, either in life or in death.
All is eternal around, nor belongeth to nation now living;
    Unto the world it belongs, unto the genius of man.
Yet, with the things that are great, with the things that for ages have
    lasted,
    Mingle the things that are small, mingle the things of a day.
Where do more daisies abound, and where do more violets nestle?
    Where are the odours of spring fresher and sweeter exhaled?
Well might the poet, who now himself in this garden is buried,
    Say that it made one in love even with Death to be here.

IV.

Even as men have made use of her ruins gigantic as quarries,
    Forming, from out of their store, structures imposing and new,
So, as to things of the mind, is Rome th' inexhaustible quarry
    Whence, as the ages have passed, nations their needs have supplied.
Languages, States and their laws, institutions enduring and splendid,
    Sciences, letters and arts, out of the wreck have been formed.
Often the fanciful poet Propertius, when Rome in her glory
    Stood, and the things that are dust shone in their splendour intact,
Loved to look back to the past, and paint to himself the great city
    As, ere Æneas arrived, nothing but hillock and grass;
Many a spot could I show you to-day, where all has reverted:
    That which a city became, grass has become once again.
Orchards deserted surround us, and patches of grass unfrequented,
    Filled with the flowers of spring, scenting the air all around.
This is the Esquiline hill; and the shout of the workman whose shovel
    Strikes on some treasure of art, startles at moments the air.

Something the men have discovered, and eagerly gather about it;
    Something which, lit by the sun, sparkles with many a tint.
Lo, on uplifting the turf, a pavement of marble mosaic,
    Rich in its varied design, near to the surface appears;
Tricked by a little frail verdure, we saw in this spot but the present,
    Yet, in a world which is old, that which we trod was the past.

V.

Endless, O Rome, is thy teaching! thy sight, of itself, is a lesson:
    Who can regard thee unmoved, though for an hour, not more?
Who ever tarried in vain in the shadow of temple and circus,
    Where, on the ground at your feet, moulder the fragments of frieze
Where, in the earth that is hallowed, it may be that statues are hidden,
    Which, at the zenith of art, Phidias or Polyclete wrought?
There, as you sit in the twilight, with Time as your only companion,
    Under your eyes are displayed History's views that dissolve.
Grand is the saddening series. Faint, in the distance of ages,
    Empires come into view, taking consistence and shape:
Brighter and brighter they grow, until, with a splendid effulgence,
    Filling the whole of the scene, still for a moment they stand;
Then they unnoticed decline, and fainter becoming and fainter,
    Melt into others away, leaving behind but a name.

ABOUT OVID.

HE is a sorry philosopher, who to the days that are recent,
  Limits his sympathies all, hearing no cries from the past.
Time has but little to do with what is eternally human;
  That which went forth from the heart, ne'er for the heart is unfit.
Think'st thou thy woe of to-day will be deeper or truer to-morrow
  Than in a thousand years hence? Time does not lessen a fact,
Nor can it deaden a cry of grief unaffected and simple;
  Let but the words be preserved, in them the pathos remains.
Only a day or two back, I lighted by chance on the passage
  (Read and re-read in the schools, hackneyed enough, in good sooth),
Where, in the *Tristia*, Ovid recurs to the night of his exile,
  When his last moments in Rome swiftly were gliding away.
Fresh was my mind, and long free from the deadening work of the
      schoolroom;
  Straight went the words to the heart, straight through the centuries
      dead.
Vivid, indeed, is the scene, with touching simplicity painted:
  Almost the moonlight we see, bathing the city that sleeps.
" When, of that saddest of nights, the picture uprises before me,
  Which was the last, very last, spent in the city by me:
When I remember that night, on which I left all that was dear,
  Down from my eyes, on my cheek, trickles a tear even now.

Then had relapsed into silence the voice of men and of watch-dogs ;
    High was the Moon in the sky, guiding her coursers of night.
As I looked up to her face, and she showed me the Capitol's structures,
    Closely adjacent to which stood all in vain our home :
Deities all, I exclaimed, who dwell in the neighbouring places,
    Temples which I, with these eyes, never again shall behold ;
Ay, and ye gods that I leave, who belong to Quirinus's city,
    Let me, before I depart, bid you for ever farewell."

PASQUA.

Weird old town medieval, say, why wert thou placed by thy founders
    Thus out of reach of mankind, high on the Apennines' crest ?
Say, were the chestnut-clad slopes, the well-watered valleys, less tempting,
    When, in a far-distant time, rose thy high circular walls ?
Never since then hast thou changed; thy houses are ever the self-same,
    All in thy ramparts is old ; man has alone been renewed.
Once a strong mountain republic, and now a town peopled by peasants,
    Who, with a simple respect, cling to their homes of the past.
Nought but an arduous bridle-path leads to the bleak mountain plateau,
    Yet do thy houses of stone tell of a pride that is gone.
Poor old vestige of time, the birthplace of glories forgotten,
    Ill does thy high airy seat suit our wealth-seeking days ;
Those who inhabit La Rocca must live in the ways of their fathers ;
    Humbly, by primitive means, mainly by manual work.
He who aspires to more must stifle the treacherous instinct,
    Or from his birthplace depart, never again to return.
Famed is the place for its women ; their beauty for miles is a proverb ;
    Though, in that Apennine tract, many a village might boast.
Race of the Apuan Alps, the fairest that speaks the pure Tuscan,
    Who can thy vigour surpass ? who to thy beauty attain ?
Curly, light-brown is the hair, and yet the complexion is southern,
    Warm as the tints of the hills, lit by the fast-sinking sun.

Watch we the women at work in the shade, in the heat of the noon-tide,
  Out in the quaint little square, or on the steps of the church,
Sorting the golden cocoons, or twirling the flax on the spindle,
  Singing in cadence a chant, nasal, metallic, and strange.
Bare are their arms and their feet; at most on the latter is poised,
  Just on the tip of the toe, lightly the white wooden clog.
Look at the maidens that stand, out there by the murmuring fountain,
  Patiently waiting their turn, till they the water can get.
See on their heads how they balance the urn-shaped pitcher of copper,
  As, with the step of a queen, slowly they turn from the spring.
Beauty they have and to spare; but one who is fairer than they are—
  One who is left to herself—fain would I show to you now.
Long might you search at La Rocca, and never discover her equal;
  Pasqua, come show us thy face; Pasqua, come show us thy smile!
There all alone is she sitting, within the dark shade of the house-door;
  Well does the time-blackened stone circle her form like a frame.
Busy her hands and her eyes in the making of lace on a cushion;
  Neatly the threads she directs, nimbly the pins she removes.
Snowy, though coarse, is her shift, and low from her shoulders it falleth;
  Prudery, turn up thy eyes; God did not make her for thee.
Dark blue the skirt that she wears, bedraping her limbs in their
    roundness;
  Naked her arms and her feet, nut-brown and braided her hair.
Not with her lace are her thoughts, for see how she frequently, pausing,
  Lifts up her eyes from the work, dreamily looks into space;
Where is the prince that shall come to marry this rare village beauty?
  Fairy tale, follow thy course! Poesy, fashion her fate!
Poor the chance of the girl if quickly the prince do not fetch her;
  Worldliness under the thatch, as in the palace, resides;
Show me the farmer of prudence would marry a portionless maiden;
  Beggars may marry for love; peasants must marry for fields.
Pasqua is poor, alas! and earneth a scanty subsistence,
  Making her beautiful lace, selling it down in the plain.

Many a summer has passed since her father abandoned La Rocca,
  Seeking America's shores, leaving his wife and his child.
Lapo, for that was his name, was owner of one of the houses
  Which, in the quaint little place, lean on the turreted wall.
Little of wealth he possessed, but yet, for his wants, all sufficient;
  Chestnuts and vines on the slope, which with his hand he could till;
While in a manner monotonous, far from unhappy, the seasons
  Passed one by one o'er his head, gently increasing his store.
Lapo would sometimes descend, but only to spend a few hours,
  Into the towns of the plain, where there were markets or fairs.
One day, big with his fate, that he thus had come down from La Rocca,
  Tools for his vineyard to buy, and at the inn had put up,
Where, in the heat of the day, the peasants were wont to assemble,
  Playing at *morra* or cards, ere they their purchases made ;
All who were there were engaged discussing about California,
  Where you had only to stoop, gold to pick up in the street ;
Great was just then the sensation produced by the newly-found gold-
    fields.
  Listen wherever you would, men talked of nothing but gold.
Gold lay in heaps at the surface, in nuggets as large as potatoes ;
  Nay, there were lumps in the ground larger than pumpkins by
    far.
Open to all was the country : the cousin of one of the speakers
  Left for the diggings next week ; great were his faith and his hope :
Silent and gaping sat Lapo, imbibing the wondrous description,
  Holding uneaten his cheese, leaving untasted his wine ;
Where was that country ? he asked ; but no one could give him the
    answer ;
  Far, very far, that was all—somewhere right over the sea.
Deeply absorbed in his thoughts was Lapo the ignorant peasant,
  When, on his way to his home, through the rich valleys he passed
Picturing unto himself those strange, inexhaustible gold-fields.
  Little he looked to the right, little he looked to the left ;

Yet all around him was gold; the gold of his own native country.
Labour, the mother of wealth, strewed it with liberal hand;
Golden the waves of the corn, just ripe for the rich second harvest;
Golden the fruit on the trees, golden the load of the vine;
Strung round each cottage in garlands, the maize hung in ponderous ingots,
Fashioned in Nature's own mint, out of her finest red gold;
Out in the gardens the maidens the yellow floss silk were preparing
Leading the soft wavy gold lightly with dexterous hand.
What was not golden, the sun, departing in splendour, was gilding.
Peasant, where was thy soul? Traveller, where were thy eyes?
During the following weeks, the peasant strangely was altered,
Little he cared for his work, which he had hitherto loved.
Oftener far than before, now into the plain he descended,
Staying away many days, leaving his fields all untilled;
Oft was he strangely depressed, oft was he strangely elated,
Never serene and content, as he had formerly been.
Vainly he fought with himself, and strove to forget California;
To it his thoughts would revert, as to the candle the moth.
Little by little the truth, and all that would come in the future,
Dawned on the mind of his wife, filling with anguish her soul.
Soon it was known in the village that Lapo had sold half the vineyard,
Only leaving unsold that which belonged to his wife.
Who does not seek to ennoble the motive of wrong or of folly?
Lapo was kindly of heart, all for his loved ones should be;
Pasqua, the child of his heart, should have a magnificent dower,
All at La Rocca should sit, sharing her rich marriage feast.
Quickly passed by the last days, spent in remonstrance, entreaty;
Who can deter the resolved, or the persuaded dissuade?
Year after year passed away, nor brought any knews of the wand'rer;
Hope was their friend for a time: slowly it turned to despair,
As, with the lapse of the summers, Pasqua grew fairer and fairer,
So did her mother decline, drooping and drooping away.

Broken the stem of her life when bearing its choicest flowers,
　　After the blow had been struck, never it blossomed again ;
Not all the sunshine of Pasqua could waken up hope or exertion ;
　　Far were her heart and her mind, over an ocean unknown.
Small were the fields that were left ; but they needed a constant exertion.
　　Broken in heart and in health, ill could she manage the work.
Debt upon debt was contracted, and pitiless relatives sued her :
　　Seized was the humble estate, hunger stared in at the door.
Then were they solely supported by Pasqua the beautiful maiden ;
　　Quickly she learnt to make lace, working from morning to night ;
Pasqua, the beautiful child, turned into a beautiful woman ;
　　None that La Rocca could show stood by her side unimpaired.
There, by a strange village irony, all named her Pasqua the Dowered ;
　　Even the children would cry, " Wilt thou not give us a share ? "
Sadly, nor conscious of malice, the maiden accepted the nickname ;
　　Just as the swan in the tale, living awhile with the ducks.
Never the weary fingers deserted the lace-making cushion,
　　Cheerfully earning for two, till the necessity ceased.
Azrael, angel of death, when flying one night o'er La Rocca,
　　Carried the mother away, leaving the daughter alone.
This is the story of Pasqua—of Pasqua as first I beheld her
　　Guiding the threads of her lace, nimbly removing the pins.
Many a summer has passed, nor has altered the face of La Rocca ;
　　Should you the mountain ascend, all you will find as it was.
There are the women at work in the shade, in the heat of the noontide
　　Out in the quaint little square, or on the steps of the church
Sorting the golden cocoons, or twirling the flax on the spindle,
　　Singing in cadence their chant, nasal, metallic, and strange.
There are the girls at the spring, with their urn-shaped pitchers of copper
　　Patiently waiting their turn, till they the water can get.
Pasqua alone is not there ; she long has deserted her village,
　　Seeking for work in the plain—making no longer her lace.
There, in a noisy city, she earneth her bread as a servant,
　　Now nor so young nor so fair.　Even a Pasqua must fade.

E

OUR FALLEN LEAVES.

Life has its Springs and its Autumns; and oft, as new fancies are bud-
  ding,
Softly the dead ones we hear, rustling beneath our feet.
See, all around us they lie, these leaves of the Past that are fallen;
  Can it be they that appeared lately so green and so fresh?
Faces we see with indifference, which once with emotion we followed;
  Voices fall on the ear, reaching no longer the heart;
Names that a magic possessed, are endowed with that magic no longer;
  Ties that we cherished are cut, dreams that we cherished are gone!
Places that Fancy had hallowed, we find, after years, to be common;
  If as we pass them we sigh, 'tis for our youth that has fled.
These are the leaves of the past, which, marching through life ever
  onwards,
Shaded by leaves that are green, bravely we tread under foot.
Yet it may happen at times, if we stoop, and a leaf that is withered
Gently take up in the hand, those that are green are forgot.

AN EMPTY SHELL.

As there are creatures of Ocean that dwell in the shells of the perished,
    So do the children of men dwell in their homes of the past.
What are their houses but shells, which belong not to one generation;
    Shells into which they were born, shells that at death they vacate?
Yes, in a shell of the past, man liveth his life of the present;
    Poor ephemeral guest, e'en in the house that is his.
Fondly he clings to the home that his fathers have left him to dwell in,
    Leaving it then to his sons, as it was left unto him.
This is the nature of man; but man is in all inconsistent;
    Halls that are strong and are fair often he strangely deserts—
Nay, these are often the fairest, too fair and too splendid, it may be.
    For an impoverished State, or an impoverished Prince;
Or, with the progress of time, the State or the Family endeth,
    Leaving a palace behind, empty, to tell what it was.
Old as the building may be, it seems to belong to the present,
    When there are heard in its walls murmurs of everyday life.
When it is needed by men. But when it is closed and deserted,
    Left to the worm and the moth, then to the Past it belongs:
Then on the place so abandoned there settles a spirit of sadness:
    He who enters it then seems to re-enter the Past:
Then there attaches to all a faint indescribable perfume,
    Something like that which belongs unto a flower preserved.
Many a palace I know, of Elector or stately Prince-Bishop
    Which is inhabited now only by ghosts of the Past;

Vestiges left of the day when the smallest of Germany's Princes,
　In a Versailles of his own, mimicked the grandeur of Louis.
These are the Elegist's haunts, the places he loves to repeople,
　Calling again into life all that is dust and is dead.
Nymphenthal, thou, above all, art the type of these shells that are empty;
　Thou, above all, art the place dear to the Elegist's heart.
Here, where the vases and statues are green from the drippings of elm-
　　trees,
　Or by the hedges of yew, clipped but unfrequently now,
Or by the triton-shaped fountains that bubble and murmur in sadness,
　Oft is he met with alone—no, very far from alone;
For, all around him are moving, unseen by the eyes of the vulgar,
　Figures old-fashioned and quaint, well fitting in with the spot;
Beauties who grew to be grey, and gay cavaliers whose descendants
　Seldom set foot in the place, now so deserted and dull.
Yes, for the Elegist still, the Electress, in powder and patches,
　Walks with her ladies at times, here in these gardens ill kept.
Still, on the broad gravelled paths, when in autumn there rustles for
　　others
　Nought but the leaf that is dead, rustle her garments for *him*.
Poor forgotten Electress: her picture is there in the palace,
　Looking so young and so fresh; ay, and so happy and bright.
Yet was her fate most unhappy, and common enough to princesses
　Loving below them in rank, loved in return, but in vain;
Wedded by fate to a man, whose delight was the drilling of soldiers,
　Lonely she wasted her youth, lonely 'mid pomp and display—
Seeking her life to ennoble, and shedding a sunshine around her,
　Striving to warm into love hearts that were colder than hers—
Nothing remains of her now but her name and the beautiful portrait,
　Which on the empty old rooms wastes unadmired its smile.—
Seldom the doors are unlocked, for seldom the visitor asks it;
　Those who are lords of the place seem to avoid its sight.

AT THE DOOR OF THE JUSTICE MILITAIRE.

VERSAILLES, JUNE 1871.

SLOWLY the hours pass by for the weary wives of the prisoners,
  Who since the earliest morn sit on the staircase of stone,
Patiently waiting their turn, at the door of the dreaded court-martial,
  Which at Versailles is engaged sorting the captives new made.
Vast is the number of prisoners, thirty thousand and upwards,
  Slowly the sorting proceeds, great though the diligence be.
Slowly the hours pass by, for the women who sit on the staircase,
  Longer and longer the shades grow on the opposite wall.
Many from Paris have walked, in the dust, with a load of provisions ;
  Some with a child at the breast—all with a load at their hearts.
Great is the love of these women, and given in noble repayment
  Often for years of neglect, often perhaps for a blow.
Ugly are most of the prisoners, and uglier still since their capture,
  Covered with dust and unshaved, stinted of food and of sleep ;
Yet there are women who love them, and who in the moment of danger
  Bravely come to their help, thinking but little of self ;
Bringing them linen and bread, and collecting in haste testimonials,
  Which their guilt to disprove, or to extenuate, tend.
Fast is the sun disappearing behind the tall roof of the palace ;
  Soft through the window it shines on to the women who wait.

Lightly the twilight is spreading its mantle of grey o'er the landscape;
  Yet are the women still there, bent on their mission of good.
Little by little their number has dwindled to scarcely a dozen;
  Less than an hour remains, then will no more be received;
See, they are growing uneasy and frequently asking the sentry;
  Little he knows or will tell, save that it closes at eight.
Those who have not had a hearing must take up their places to-morrow,
  Waiting again on the steps, as they have waited to-day.
Gently the sentry explains that the doors are about to be fastened;
  Slowly the women move off, bearing their burden of woe.

THE FIELD GRAVE.

SCARCELY have died on the ear the cannons' last lingering echoes,
  Boom upon boom in the plain; Fancy still hears them recur.
O'er, but just o'er is the war, and Germany's children, victorious,
  Homeward are wending their way, leaving their dead to their fate.
Smouldering still are the fires that War and Rebellion have lighted;
  France from her numberless wounds bleeds unassisted and weeps.
Ruin and wreck all around; and I, a stranger unnoticed,
  Sit by these nameless mounds, earliest of mourners, and muse;
" Here are three Frenchmen interred, and here two Prussians are lying;"
  This is their epitaph brief, telling the simplest of tales;
See, on a small wooden cross the words are inserted in pencil,
  Almost effaced by the rain, soon they will quite disappear.
Bitterest epitaph this, that asks for no tribute, and tells not
  Unto their mothers the place where they are now to be sought.
Fate, thou art ever ironical! Wherefore this mockery cruel?
  Couldst thou not bury apart those who in life had been foes?
Barely a month has elapsed since these men felt the bitterest hatred;
  Now they approach and they touch; almost each other they kiss.
Lone are the fields at this hour, and only a white-headed peasant
  Stops to look on this grave, common to friend and to foe.
Something the ear cannot catch, he mutters as onwards he passes;
  Is it a prayer for the one, or for the other a curse?

Rather the latter I fear. But I, who am foeman of neither,
    Ere I depart from the ground, fain would do honour to both.
Both did their duty and fell, and both are now equally nameless;
    Chaucing to dwell on the path crossed by the Chariot of War.
Mourners at home they may have, and hearts that are sinking with
    anguish;
    Here by the place where they lie, only a stranger can sit,
None that in life they had known. And so, if the stranger should
    happen
    Somewhat a poet to be, let him their Elegy write.

A SUFFERER.

War I have seen and its victims: the wounded slowly emerging,
    One by one, from their beds, seeking the quickening sun;
Girded no more with the sword, but learning to manage their crutches,
    Stopping at intervals short, wistfully looking around;
Spectres, haggard and pale, and armless and legless, whom nature,
    Using the breeze of the spring, gently was trying to cure.
Yet these victims of war, thus crawling about in the sunshine,
    Are not the sole who drag on, maimed in the morning of life.
Other cripples there are, whose story is sadly inglorious,
    Not stricken down at a blow, living for years in suspense:
Wearing no medal or cross, and knowing nor brevet nor pension:
    Maimed by the Powers above, not by the engines of men.
Few cast a glance on the wretches sustaining a combat unequal,
    Yielding by inches the ground, doomed to a certain defeat;
Cheered by no bugle or drum, led on by no fluttering standard,
    Hearing not Victory's shout, as in the battle they sink;
Bed is their battle-field dull, their witness the nurse and the doctor;
    Patient and brave though they be, men have no laurels for *them*.
Yes, there are many like this; and especially one at this moment
    Maybe I have in my thoughts; often I see him, alas!
Lifted by men on a chair, and with gentleness placed in a carriage,
    Just like a victim of war; only no glory is his.

Now he but seldom complains; but who of the struggles has knowledge
　　Which by this youth were sustained, ere he accepted his lot?
Short is the story indeed.　The youth was of temper too ardent;
　　Talents he knew he possessed such as led men to success;
Yet not unworthy his aims; and pure was his youthful ambition;
　　Nought but the great and the good found in his wishes a place.
Home and its sweets he abandoned, and mixed in the world's compe-
　　　　tition;
　　Others he passed in the race; destined he seemed for a prize.
Work he desired and loved, and occasions he sought for distinction;
　　Only too many there came—all was too dearly bought—
Then by degrees imperceptible, fell o'er his pathway a shadow,
　　Seen and suspected by none, darkening daily his life.
Then came the weeks of despair: the walk that grew shorter and shorter
　　Steadily, day by day, till he could take it no more.
Yet he the secret preserved.　And then came that wildest of struggles,
　　Fought with a foe all unseen, only to keep on his feet.
Bound half divine to the earth, man clings to his physical powers
　　Hard as the sailor that drowns clings to the wreck of his ship.
Fiercely he strives to retain, when one of these powers essential,
　　Given by Nature herself, bids him eternal adieu;
Only when all is too late, does the wretch for the commonest blessing,
　　Just when it slips from his grasp, feel this ineffable love.
Then for an hour's delay, a year of his life would he barter,
　　Measuring only too well all that awaits him of woe.
Yet when the loss is complete, he subsides into patience and sadness,
　　Bearing his burden in peace, writhing in spirit no more;
Helpless and guiltless he lives, and the worthiest parts of his being
　　Grow and develop with time, bearing a fruit that is sweet.
Higher he looks for the good which the world can no longer afford
　　　　him;
　　Less of a man than before, nearer the angels he stands.

A WOODLAND ELEGY.

NATURE I love to depict: the woods and their shade evanescent.
  Filled with ephemeral life, filled with ephemeral song;
Village and homestead secluded; their occupants dull, unambitious,
  Living a life of routine old as the earth that they till;
Ay, and the murmuring stream, and the peasant girl sitting beside it,
  Waiting a step she well knows, dreaming her dream of a day;
All that is simple and good, and filled with a poetry homely;
  All that is fair and must die; all that was fair and is dead.
Nature is constantly dying, but ageth not, and her beauty
  Suffers from time no impair: such as she was she is now.
Yet, in my fancy, at times her beauty appears in the present
  Less than it was in the past: duller the tints have become.
Strange that boyhood's coasts, from which I am rapidly drifting,
  Clearer and fairer become even as farther I get!
Strange that these landscapes Italian, of which I was once so enamoured,
  Serve but to call to my mind those of the duskier north!
Often my thoughts will revert to the woods which I knew in my boy-
    hood;
  Little likely, alas! ever to see them again.
Beech-woods of foliage translucent, bestrewn with the shells of the
    beech-nuts,
  Where you the squirrel may see, darting like light o'er the path.

Where, as you walk and look up to the new-born green in the sunshine,
    Crackle the twigs that are dead, tinder-like, under your feet.
More than one land have I seen, and carried away of their beauties
    Much that unbidden, at times, knocks at the door of the heart.
Yet hath he not to go far who seeketh for beauty; it lieth
    Round the corner for all, if they have eyes and can see.
England, country of elms—of elms that are spreading and leafy:
    England, country of lanes; soft undulatory land,
Dotted with square-towered churches, that Time has adorned and has
    hallowed;
    Traversed by streams which, unheard, glide in the shade of the
    boughs;
Open to all are thy beauties, to all who can walk, and can clamber
    Over a stile, and, as yet, walk unescorted by Care.
Sweet, above all, are the walks in England's beautiful park-land,
    Under the trees that are tall, over the turf that is soft;
Where, in the dells on the grass, are the dark-green rings which the
    fairies
    Leave for the wonder of men, after their gambols at night;
Where, as you stop on your way and peep through the wooden enclosures,
    Deer, dark-eyed and tame, come to the bars for a pat;
Or 'tis the long-legged foals, who start and scamper a circle
    Round their dams as you pass; then of a sudden they stop.
And in the distance is seen, 'mid the trees, a mansion ancestral.
    Brightly its windows the while flash in the fast-setting sun.
Scenery quiet like this, more than that which is grand and romantic,
    Speaks to the Elegist's soul, waking the best of his thoughts;
Scenery soft as his mood. For he knows nor invective nor rapture;
    Sober and pensive, his strain stirs not the passions of men.
Nature for me has most charm in what is her moment elegiac;
    When she brings home to the mind all that is fleeting and fair.
Know ye the dreamy and soft, and scarcely definable feeling,
    Tinged with a quiet regret, yet not unhappy withal,

Which our autumn imparts, in a walk through the well - wooded
country;
When, without omen of ill, rustles the leaf under foot;
When the mind that is calm is possessed by the beauty of Nature,
Yet is aware of a voice telling of mutable things?
This is Elegy latent; and he who in Nature can feel it,
Knoweth a poetry sweet—sweeter than any in books.

AN OLD COAT.

Each has his own superstitions, and I have my fancies like others :
  One is about my old coats; scarcely I know how it came.
Nor do I know, dear Reader, which you are likely to give it,
  Whether a smile or a sigh : all on your humour depends.
When I give up an old coat, it seems as if then I were losing
  All of a sudden the years which with that coat I have passed ;
Older I suddenly feel ; for the life which is daily expended
  (This is my fancy as well) clings to the folds of the coat.
What has become of the youth of which pitiless Powers deprive us,
  Hour by hour, alas ?   May it not lurk in the coat ?
Know not the coat the emotions, the hope and the fear and the pleasure ?
  Was it not close to the heart, feeling the least of its throbs ?
Only this morning, by chance, I fell on a coat long discarded ;
  One I had worn at a time when I was happier than now.
As I looked on it, those days, and myself, as I now am no longer,
  Clearly, too clearly ! rose up ; just for a minute, no more.
Almost I then could have cried to this spectre thus suddenly met with :
  Give me the life thou hast drained ; mine it was then and 'tis now !
Where are the years that I gave thee ? the years that I left in thy
    lining ?
  Where are the youth and the health ?   Where are the hopes unful-
    filled ?
'Twas but a shabby old coat ; but I thought as I looked on the edges,
  Thready and white, of the sleeves : this which is worn was my life.

ADVICE.

Boy, thy nature is good, though somewhat too ardent thy temper;
  Why do I see thee so oft, lonely, discouraged, and sad?
More and more every day thou keepest aloof from thy fellows,
  Thinking of nought on this earth save thy ambitious designs.
More and more every day I see thee neglecting thy pastimes,
  Even those that were once dearest unto thy heart;
Working from morning till night, nor stopping to look on creation.
  Jaded in body and mind, knowing of neither the sweets.
Life is a garden immense, one half of whose fruits are a semblance:
  Art thou not plucking the false, leaving untasted the true?
He who would live to succeed must live as if life were eternal,
  Knowing both pleasure and work, giving its measure to each.
Fame is not taken by storm, but surrenders with time unto merit;
  He who can wait for his day, holdeth the game in his hands.
Abler thou art than the crowd; but dangers unknown to the vulgar—
  Dangers for body and mind—lie in Ability's way.
Happy and safe Mediocrity, knowing no path but the beaten,
  Seeking no heights that allure—skirting no hidden abyss—
Playing a little with Vice, while holding the fingers of Virtue—
  Guided by instinct, not thought: almost I envy thy lot!
Fain would I spare thee, O Boy, the bitter and sickening lesson,
  Which, with a temper like thine, Fate but too readily gives;

Only I fear 'tis decreed, that each for himself in Fate's schoolroom,
　Learning life's lesson must sit, earning the prize or the rod.
Fain would I warn thee in time; for maybe a similar error,
　Cost me, while youth slipt away, much of the joy of life.
Yes, the future too much, the present too little, I cared for,
　Thinking too much of success, missing life's real delights;
Deeming the work of the mind alone to be noble and worthy;
　Searching all wisdom in books; knowing nor leisure nor rest.
Yet there were times even then, when a better philosophy entered
　Transiently into my heart, yielding the healthiest fruit.
Outwards then, and not inwards, the eyes of the mind were directed;
　Filled was the present with good,—nought in the future I sought;
Looking on Nature with love, on Nature the good and the fleeting,
　While there was youth in the heart giving the power to feel.
Yes, there are moments in life, when Destiny's coursers that bear us
　Whither we know not, away, slacken their terrible pace;
When on the road of existence, we look not ahead, but around us,
　Holding the reins with loose hand, feeling secure for a while,
When, as we look on the world through which we too fast have been
　　hurried,
　Nothing but beauty we see—beauty serene and divine.
Few are the moments of respite, when thus on the weary journey,
　Man can enjoy the scene; soon do they come to an end:
Scarce have the coursers relaxed, when, lashed by invisible spirits,
　Wildly their race they resume, bearing us helpless away.

SOLVILLE.

SPRING, light-footed and young, has stolen a march on old Winter:
  See here he comes on his way, scattering blossoms and buds.
Soft is the kiss of the sun; and the breeze which is laden with per-
      fumes,
  Stolen from meadows and woods, daintily kisses the cheek.
Such were the mornings of Solville, where spring was for ever the
      master;
  Often I think of them now, under a different sky.
Often I think of them now, when old Winter bends over his embers.
  Bloodless and shrunken and sad, warming his tremulous hands.
There, when in lands of the North, the dull leaden clouds lower heavy
  Over the desolate plains, leafless and hard with the frost,
Softly the sun, all unclouded, looks down on an Eden of flowers,
  Softly the calm tepid sea breaks on the sweet-scented shore.
There be the home of the greyish-green olive; the orange and citron,
  Heavily weighted with gold, fill all the gardens around.
Aloes gigantic and fleshy, or hedges untrimmed of geranium,
  Border the mountainous paths, where in the shade of a pine,
Reddish and scaly of trunk, or in that of a feathery date-palm,
  Taking your seat on a stone, you can look down on the town
And on the placid blue sea, as it lies in its sunniness lake-like:
  Over it swiftly, at times, hurries a ripple immense.

F

Yes, I think often of Solville, reviewing its numberless beauties,
    Musing on years that are gone, calling old faces to mind.
Who has not got, at a distance, a world he no longer belongs to,
    Doing without him, alas! only too easily now;
Some little world often thought of, but which now has forgotten him
    wholly,
    Where, once for ever interred, lie the best years of his life?
If the occasion should happen to come, perhaps it is wiser
    Not to revisit the place: let it belong to the past.
Sadness sufficient the echoes possess, which at intervals reach us,
    When we expect it the least, waking up memories dead.
If from that world long forsaken, somebody suddenly dropping,
    With the same face as of old, says to us, " What, is it you?"
Then there comes over us straightway a strange undefinable feeling,
    Something which jars and is wrong, breaking the current of time,
Which every one of us feels, when, close by the side of the Present,
    Sits uninvited the Past, old and familiar of face.
If he should mention some change, that new houses, for instance, are
    building,
    Or that the trees have been felled, and that the aspect is changed,
Something like anger we feel, that strangers should venture to alter
    That which is memory's own, taking its beauty away.
If he should tell us, by chance, that the children are children no longer,
    Or that the elders are dead, or that new faces are there,
Quickly a sadness comes over the heart, and a sense that the river,
    Which we call Time, has flowed on; none on its bosom can moor.

THE DESERTED VILLA.

WELL does the dying old place fit in with a framework of Autumn ;
　When the wild vine on the wall turneth from green into red ;
When the far hills of Æmilia have turned to a shadowy russet ;
　When, in the plain that surrounds, sober and sad are the tints ;
When, in the fields that are bare, the smoke of the weeds that are
　　burning
Bluish and curling ascends, filling the air with a haze ;
When the tough leaves of the poplar lie flat on the path that they
　　cover,
Yellow and brilliant and smooth, glued to each other by dew ;
When the heat that is banished, but lingering still in the noontide,
　Draws from all Nature around odours autumnal and sweet ;
When every flower still left emits a faint perfume of sadness ;
　When on the world that she leaves, Beauty expiring smiles.
Beautiful villa deserted ! The hollyhocks tall and ungainly
　Lord it unchecked o'er the place ; marigolds cover the beds.
Where, in the days that are gone, the choicest flowers abounded,
　These are all that remain, these are the things that adorn.
Hens from a neighbouring farm are pecking about in the gravel
　Where, in his plumage superb, ventured the peacock alone.
Shedding its pointed leaves, an old knotted willow is weeping
　Over the wrought-iron gate, seldom or never unlocked.

Posted near to this gate, a painted earthenware soldier,
    Life-size, stands in the dress worn by Great Frederick's troops.
Poor useless old sentinel !　While thou art guarding the entrance,
    Dost thou not know that the foe taketh the house in the rear ?
Cruel Neglect is the enemy ; stealthily creeping in silence,
    Sapping and mining he comes ; soon will he reach even thee.
Mark how the wily besieger approaches the house through the garden,
    Raising weedy stockades, parallels forming of moss.
Now he reaches the walls, removing the plaster by patches,
    Leaving a stain on the stone where he but places his hand.
Deep on the light iron balconies, see how the rust he is spreading,
    Leaving no trace of the gold decking the gateway of yore ;
E'en on the realm of Time the treacherous foe is encroaching.
    Look at the sun-dial there, traced on the wall of the house :
Almost effaced are its numerals ; while, with a truth that is mournful,
    Stands written o'er it this verse, faint, but legible still :
Tempora mutantur, et nos mutamur in illis ;
    All on the dial is pale, all save the time-marking shade.
Year after year passes by, the willow renewing its pale-green
    Pointed leaves in the spring, near to the wrought-iron gate ;
Shedding them yellow in autumn, near to the earthenware sentry,
    Filling the brim of his hat, lying in heaps at his feet.
Nobody cares for the beautiful place ; but the stranger who passes
    Looks through the railings awhile, turning in sadness away.

III.

POEMS IN LYRICAL METRES

THE SONG OF THE PLASTER CAST.

In the following poem I have attempted to tell the story of a Greek statue ; not of this or of that individual copy of it,—for of nearly every great antique, antiquity alone has given us four or five copies, which in modern times have been reproduced indefinitely in marble or plaster,—but of that which constitutes the identity of the statue—which makes us say, in the presence of a plaster cast, or merely of a drawing, " This is the Discobulus of Myron," "This is the Faun of Praxiteles,"—in short, of the *form*, of the conception which arose in the mind of the sculptor, and which he, first, embodied, but which may be indefinitely repeated — *the form* which corresponds in the statue to that purely intellectual identity that makes the *Iliad* the *Iliad*, *Paradise Lost Paradise Lost*, in whichever of a hundred different editions it may be seen ; as much in the half-crown copy which we buy to-day, as in the earliest manuscript existing. This abstract *form*, and not its individual embodiment in stone or metal, is *the statue ;* and my object has been to trace the many changes of substance through which the form of a renowned Greek Venus has been handed down to us in all its identity.

I AM but an antique Form,
By Time's ever-raging Storm
Ever spared.
Even in this Plaster Cast,
Lives my beauty of the Past
Unimpaired,

For of old I was created
In an image all divine :
Aphrodité, newly risen
From the Ocean's bitter brine.

I have passed from clay to marble,
And from marble into bronze,
And to marble then reverted ;
For my antique beauty dons
Now one substance, now the other ;
And in each I have asserted
My identity to men.
Clay and bronze and marble perished,
But the statue did not die,
For its very form am I.
What the Sculptor's genius cherished,
What the Sculptor's genius gives,
That was saved, and in me lives.

Twice a thousand years have rolled
Slowly, sadly o'er my head,
And the world has long grown old,
And the tongues I heard are dead,
Since the finger of the Greek
Made the dimple in my cheek.
Nations, creeds, and arts and glories
Came, and lived, and passed away ;
But the dimple still endureth,
As upon my earliest day.
Dost thou ask me for the secret
Of my endless youth and fame ?
I will tell thee how, unaltered,
Through the centuries I came.

Greece alone could make me, Greece
In an age of strength and peace,
After Salamis was won;
When beneath his tempered sun,
Man, secure from every storm,
In the beauty of the form
Found his best and highest pleasure;
And the secret of all measure
He possessed;
When in marble he expressed
All his fancy's fair creations;
Gods of beauty, Gods of gladness,
Who, in human semblance dressed,
Ruled a world too young for sadness;
Or the motley brood of Pan,
Who, through wood and field and meadow,
In perennial riot ran.

Round the temple fair and stately,
On whose pediment I stood,
Moved a life
With beauty rife,
And rife with good.
Slowly wound the long procession
Through the temple-bordered street,
With its tall Corinthian columns
Which extended at my feet;
And a look the sun-burnt maidens
Often upwards to me cast,
As they passed,
With their load of fruits and flowers;
And the stalwart youths who followed,
In an endless cavalcade,

On their small and prancing horses,
All in colours bright arrayed ;
And the many-voiced echoes
Of the games fell on my ear,
And the shouting of the crowd,
In its exultation loud,
To this day I seem to hear.
For the marble Gods looked on,
While the Olympic race was won ;
While the noblest youths contended,
Strong of heart and lithe of limb ;
And the loud triumphal hymn,
Hailed the victor, as he wended,
In his strength and beauty splendid,
With the palm to place his name
On the sacred roll of Fame,
Which all time should fail to dim.

But that life within my sight,
Grew less strong and grew less bright,
And the art which at my birth
Reached its zenith upon earth,
Slowly, slowly, slowly waned ;
Shining with a fading splendour,
Growing softer and more tender,
Till at length,
Nought of greatness or of strength
There remained.

For it is decreed in Heaven,
That on Earth,
Seed of Death to all be given
At its birth.

All that groweth, all that greeneth,
      Must decay.
Every star must at its zenith
      Wane away.
Every fountain's rising column
      Forms a curve;
All things this commandment solemn
      Must observe.
Nought may at its zenith linger,
      But must move;
Fate with its resistless Finger
      Gives the shove.
Every art and every greatness
      Spends its force,
And in earliness or lateness
      Takes this course.

Not alone the chisel then
Was blunted in the hands of men,
As the sense of art decayed;
But the keen and shining blade,
Wrought by Freedom for the Greek,
Grew too quickly blunt and dim;
And the spirit and the limb
Both were weak.

Then the fair Hellenic islands
First the heavy thraldom knew
Of the iron-sided masters
Of a world that ever grew;
And the accents unfamiliar
Of the terser Roman tongue
Sounded on the shores, where Pindar,
The immortal, once had sung.

On the noblest works of beauty,
In the unresisting land,
On the statues that were fairest,
Fell the robbing Roman hand.
And the hard rapacious Prætors
Of the ever greedy Rome,
Dragged a marble people captive
From its beauteous island home.

Thus I left the olive hills,
And the myrtle and the bay,
And the clear and rapid rills,
Whose unceasing murmur fills
Every valley on the way,
From the centre to the strand,
Of the little Attic land
Of my birth.

And the temple-crownéd headlands,
Stretching in a silvery sea,
Warm and calm ;
And the rock-begirded islands,
Whence in noon's long dreamy hours,
Comes the scent of many flowers,
Hidden in the woods of palm.

Through the crowded Roman streets
I was dragged ;
And the soldier people bragged
Of their distant martial feats,
And the trophies they had got ;
But they felt my beauty not.

And I passed from hand to hand,
As the tardy years went by,
In the houses of the great;
And my masters made me stand,
And look down upon their state
From my pedestal on high;
Till at last, placed and displaced,
Nero's golden house I graced;
Where I saw, amid the din
Of the orgie, all the sin
Of the worlds that slowly rot;
But my soul was sullied not.

Then I left the home of Cæsar
For the round gigantic Mole,
Tomb of Hadrian eternal,
And watched the yellow Tiber roll,
E'en as rolled the flood of Ages,
Towards a distant sea unknown;
Bearing creeds and arts and nations,
Leaving me behind alone.
From the shore of Time I watched them
Pass unconscious on their way,
While my brow remained unfurrowed,
Fair as on my native day.
For the beauty of the statue,
And the beauty of the bust,
Shall endure in youth untarnished,
Till they crumble into dust.

There I stood until the day
When the giant Mole, transformed
To a fortress stern and grey,

By the northern hosts was stormed.
Underneath, and far and wide,
Surged the fierce barbarian tide,
With a loud and angry roar,
Wave on wave against us bore,
And upward dashed,
While the ram resistless crashed,
And a thousand arrows rained
On to statues, on to men,
And the stainless marble then
Deep was stained.
In their ugly pools of red
Lay the dying and the dead,
At my feet.
From their high, time-honoured seat,
Statues, wonders of the world,
Headlong from the walls were hurled,
Through the missile-blackened air,
In the madness of despair.
And the flames of war rose high,
And a lurid radiance now,
Like a deeper sunset's glow,
Filled the sky.

So the statue which, the earliest,
Bore my form in human sight,
Which had lived a thousand summers,
Perished in a single night.

But I, its essence, did not perish ;
'Twas the stone alone that died ;
For, though men may seem to conquer,
'Tis the Gods alone decide.

And a copy of my beauty
Stood beneath a golden dome,
In a long-deserted villa,
Of the dying, dying Rome.

Old was the building, by patches the plaster
Fell with the frescoes each year from the walls;
Age and desertion worked faster and faster,
Now in the silent, still beautiful halls.
Only we statues, 'mid rank vegetation,
Peopled the portico, garden, and court;
Man seldom troubled the dull desolation,
Never he gave us a look or a thought.
Down from the ceilings, on floors of mosaic,
Crumbled the cornices, hiding them fast;
Till on what lingered of beauty Archaic,
Inward the roofs fell like thunder at last.
All was now shapeless; the statues, once splendid,
Lay in the heap, from their pedestals hurled;
Gently the mould, the encroacher, all ended:
That which was beauty had passed from the world.

For a thousand years I lay,
Deep imbedded in the clay;
And the ground above the sleeper
Grew unnoticed ever deeper,
Day by day.

Men and women
Overhead
Lived their little life
Of an hour,
Like the flower

And the herb.
Beauties courted and superb
Felt decay
And passed away,
Like a breath;
Knowing nothing of the beauty,
Ever radiant,
Underneath.

And the change was great and solemn
Which had come upon the earth;
And the world's fair face had wrinkled,
Since the days which gave me birth.
Still the Sun's unwearied chariot
Crossed the ether as before;
But the young and radiant Phœbus
Held its golden reins no more.
Still the forest depths were shady,
Still were green the woodland lawns;
But they now no more were peopled
By the shy and happy fauns.
Still the streams and still the fountains
Murmured as they passed along;
But the Naiads now no longer
Turned their murmur into song.
In the fields there were no pipings,
For an unknown voice had said,
On the silent shores of Hellas,
Long ago, that Pan was dead.
In men's hearts there was no gladness;
Hushed was every sound of mirth.
But a litany incessant
Rose to Heaven from the Earth.

From the steeples, in the twilight,
Sounded now the evening bell;
And the world, no longer youthful,
Learned the meaning of a knell.
In the cloister's gloom, unloving,
Paced the morbid monk or nun,
Who a mortal sin esteemed it,
To feel young or love the Sun.
On the dark cathedral buttress,
Imps of stone with face of ape,
Carved by an ignoble chisel,
Mocked the godlike human shape,
While I, the human shape's perfection,
In the earth lay hidden deep,
Till a nobler generation
Should awake me from my sleep.

But the day arrived at last
When the secret of the past
Was disclosed;
And when men the Venus found
Who for ages in the ground
Had reposed.
And again, as at my birth,
To all corners of the earth,
Hurried Fame;
But it was decreed by Fate,
That she should not tell the great
Sculptor's name;
And though I the secret ken,
I reveal it not to men,
Nor may speak:
This alone I can impart,

G

That he reached the height of art,
And was Greek.
And a thousand reproductions
Of my beauty were sent forth,
And were scattered 'mong the nations,
East and West, and South and North.
While I stand in marble costly
In the palaces at Rome,
I am seen in humble plaster,
In the poorest artist's home.
I am not the bronze, the marble,
Nor the ivory and gold,
But the form impressed upon them,
By a mighty hand of old;
Little matters what the substance;
And my beauty of the Past,
Liveth unimpaired and splendid,
Even in a Plaster Cast.

THE EVER-YOUNG.

Beauty's forms are ever young,
Sculptured, painted, writ, or sung;
For the ages o'er them pass,
Light as breezes o'er the grass.
While grows old the human clay,
Never can they feel decay;
But the while the world grows older
Grow no duller, grow no colder,
And from their eternal truth,
Live in a perpetual youth.

Say, has Time impressed a furrow
On the marble Venus' brow?
Was she younger on the morrow
Of her birth than she is now?
Yet above that marble head
Twenty centuries have fled!
Mars a single thread of silver
Saint Cecilia's chestnut hair?
Is she older, is she colder
Than when Rafael was there?

Yet how many beauties, say,
Have since then grown old and grey !
Is our Shakespeare's Juliet older
Than the day she saw the light ?
Would not Romeo still enfold her
In his arms, as on that night ?
When a thousand years are cast
On the heap we call the Past,
Will the music of Mozart
Be less youthful for the heart ?

A PALIMPSEST.

I AM an eternal verse,
Framed in language strong and terse ;
Ye repeat and re-repeat me,
In your dull pedantic schools,
Till I lose all sense and beauty,
In the mouths of learnèd fools ;
And they know not whence they got me,
Nor the reason of my fame ;
And they ask not how, unaltered,
Through the centuries I came ;
My perfection is undying,
As the love of Man for Art ;
If by chance a Poet meets me,
Straight I reach unto his heart.

For a thousand years I lay
In a monastery grey,
Hidden under other ink,
By the men who loved to pray,
And who knew not how to think.
But a day arrived at last,
When my beauty of the past,

Young as ever and as bright,
Saw again the heavens' light;
For a cunning hand effaced
Every word above me traced
On the parchment old and shrunk,
By the Monk.

Faint the writing I was clothed in,
As I thus appeared again;
But it yet was all-sufficient
Immortality to gain.
Beauty, hid 'neath dusty layers,
Oft no sign for ages gives;
But it lives;
And the moment you release it,
Will once more enchant and conquer;
For, like Truth,
Beauty lives in endless youth.

VENUS UNBURIED.

Deep in the bosom of the patient earth,
  A statue slept;
And Time, the silent witness of her birth,
  The secret kept.

A female form, of Parian marble pure,
  A face of love,
Of radiant beauty, such as would allure
  The Gods above.

She once had stood within a lofty fane,
  In the world's youth;
A temple raised to her who holds profane
  All forms uncouth.

A stately city round the fane displayed
  Its proud array;
The city grew and flourished, then decayed,
  And passed away.   •

The ploughshare passed o'er the once busy hold
  Of lord and slave,
And on the spot the ripened corn then rolled
  Its golden wave.

A battle big with the world's fate was fought
    Above her head ;
And many bodies by her side were brought ;
    She touched the dead.

The name of victor and of vanquished passed,
    And left no trace ;
Their very nations' names were wiped at last
    From the earth's face.

New creeds, new tongues, new states, new arts arose ;
    'Twas but to fall,
And still the statue, in her deep repose,
    Outlived them all.

A forest grew where once the rustling breeze
    The corn had stirred ;
And o'er the sleeper browsed beneath the trees
    An antlered herd.

In endless line acorn from oak, and oak
    From acorn sprung ;
But still no sound the sleeping goddess woke,
    For ever young.

At last the forest dwindled down to earth,
    And passed away ;
All save a single oak of mighty girth,
    All gnarled and grey.

The children wild, who, round the giant played
    With merry dance,
Turned into lovers meeting in its shade,
    With furtive glance.

Then into old folk, white with years and care,
 All bent and shrunk;
Who sat and watched their children's children there,
 Play round its trunk.

The world was old, and had no memory now
 Of its own youth;
And still the statue slept with radiant brow,
 As pure as Truth.

One day men came with rope and axe, to fell
 The giant oak;
It died, as giants die, resisting well
 Stroke upon stroke.

And as it reeled and fell with thundering sound,
 The earth was cleft;
And where the roots had fastened in the ground,
 A chasm left.

One of the men peeped o'er the brink, but fled
 In wild alarm,
And swore a form had beckoned from the dead,
 With ghostly arm.

The others laughed, and then the chasm scanned,
 And there beheld
A lovely form, that with its marble hand
 The rootlets held.

And so the statue saw the light again
 Of heaven above;
And smiled on man, as in the distant Past,
 The smile of love.

So smiled soft Cypris, daughter of the Wave,
    When, at her birth,
She wrung her hair, and by her presence gave
    New life to earth.

All men from North and South, and West and East,
    The statue saw:
Prince, artist, poet, philosopher and priest,
    And man of law.

And each man owned, as on that form he gazed,
    The force of love;
And felt his soul by heavenly power raised
    To spheres above.

They placed her in a stately hall, away
    From sounds uncouth;
To tell her story of a distant day,
    In the world's youth.

When Gods as men in every myrtle grove
    Of Hellas trod;
And man, though proud of being man, yet strove
    To be a God.

When man, though fair, imagined fairer still
    The human form;
And gave to marble life's celestial thrill,
    And impulse warm;

When life and art were one harmonious whole
    To every Greek;
And man in all things found a hidden soul,
    And made it speak.

THE SECRET OF THE BUSENTO.

Deep beneath the flowing river
　　Sleeps the great Barbarian King,
While his requiem for ever
　　Overhead the waters sing.

There from man by nature guarded,
　　Was he laid in days of old,
In a triple bier enshrouded,
　　Wrought of silver, bronze, and gold.

Say, Busento, thou its keeper,
　　Where lies Alaric the Goth?
Thou hast sworn to hide the sleeper?
　　Time absolves thee of thy oath.

In the dead of night they brought him
　　To the startled river-bank;
While the world still living thought him,
　　They the coffined monarch sank.

By the torches' light they laid him
　　Deep within its rocky bed,

And a last farewell they bade him,
　Him the greatest of their dead.

Ere the pearly light of morning
　On the little party broke,
The Arian Chiefs a word of warning
　To the listening River spoke :

" Our nation's richest treasure
　To thy bosom we confide ;
Let thy depths no stranger measure,
　But the King for ever hide.

" As thy water onward dashes,
　Let it keep his tomb from shame ;
In thy charge we leave his ashes,
　In the world's his endless fame."

Thus in manner strange and hurried,
　Under night's protecting wing,
Those stern Gothic warriors buried
　Alaric their mighty King.

As the stream's retarded current
　Rolled o'er his eternal home,
So the great barbaric torrent
　Rolled on o'er the grave of Rome.

Goth and Vandal, Sueve and Lombard,
　Hun and Alan, wave on wave,
None of all their kings unnumbered
　Had as grand or safe a grave.

Guardian of a lonely glory,
   Well hast thou the secret kept,
Fourteen centuries of story,
   Undisturbed the Goth has slept.

Noble river, none could firmer
   Keep his plighted word than thou;
Alone the poet in thy murmur
   Hears the name of Alaric now.

THE VAULT OF THE ESCURIAL.

Within a dark sepulchral vault,
  In death Spain's monarchs lay,
Around a lofty crucifix
  In grand and dread array.

For twice ten years no step had waked
  The hollow echoes there;
Upon its hinge no door had turned
  To let in other air.

But lo! down yonder steps descends
  A King[1] with stifled breath:
That rapid flight of steps that kings
  Descend not save in death.

The moving torches flickering high
  His haggard face expose:
He comes to view the vault where soon
  He shall himself repose.

[1] Charles II. of Spain.

Amid the tranquil dwellers there
  He seeks for one beloved;
The wife whom death had, youthful still,
  In beauty's pride removed.

Unchanged by death's all-changing hand,
  In seeming sleep she lies;
While, oh! how changed the face of him
  That stares with straining eyes!

A single moment thus he gazed
  Upon her upturned face,
Then, raving and blaspheming, fled
  In madness from the place.

PIETRO MICCA.

AUGUST 30, 1706.

"There is no time to lay the train !
 The French are pouring in !
Away, away ! 'tis all in vain,
 And nought can save Turin !"

Like bloodhounds suddenly at fault,
 The sappers stood in doubt :
They heard from that dark bastion-vault
 The foe's exulting shout;

They heard, upon the upper floor,
 A sound of many feet;
The French were thundering at the door,
 To cut off their retreat.

'Twas then the sapper Micca said
 Unto the other two :—
"Ye see the train could ne'er be laid;
 Without a train we'll do.

"The naked match will do as well,
  And I will be the man;
The French are on us! quick! farewell!
  Escape while still ye can."

His fellow-soldiers wondering heard
  His speech with bated breath.
Small time there was to speak a word;
  They left him to his death.

Yet, one upon his steps returned,
  To shake his purpose wild;
And bade him, ere the match he burned,
  Give thought to wife and child.

But Micca dragged him from the spot,
  And cried, " 'Twill be too late !
Run, while the minutes thou hast got,
  Or thou shalt share my fate !"

The man obeyed; and one by one
  The fatal minutes fled,
And Micca, with his match alone,
  Could hear the French o'erhead.

He heard them working at the wall ;
  Two companies were there.
Himself, the bastion, and them all,
  He hurled into the air !

All, all into the sky were hurled,
  And as a fiery rain,
Upon the rent and quivering world,
  Descended back again.

11

And then a silence filled the air,
  A silence strange and long;
Afraid the birds that morning were,
  To sing their morning song.

Above the town there hung, up high,
  A single cloud of smoke,
Which slowly sailed across the sky,
  As soft Aurora woke.

It passed away.   All looked the same
  The sun in splendour rose.
No vestige of that deed of flame,
  Its author or his foes !

But time was gained by Micca's deed ;
  The French were beaten down ;
And Prince Eugene arrived and freed
  The long-beleaguered town.

IV.

TRANSCRIPTS

THE season has now vanished which had made
Into ripe fruit the blossoms it had found ;
Few are the leaves that on the bough have stayed ;
But in the thinnéd woods strewn on the ground,
They make a rustling, when across the glade
The huntsman goes : few steps like many sound.
The beast to hide its wandering track may try,
But goes ill hidden through the branches dry.

'Mid leafless trees the cheerful bay is seen,
As well as Cypris' shrub of pleasant smell ;
The fir-tree on the whitish hills is green,
And bends beneath the snow that lately fell ;
The cypress-tree doth still a few birds screen ;
With adverse winds the strong pine struggles well :
The lowly juniper sharp-leaféd stands,
And pricketh not, when pluckt with dexterous hands.

The olive-tree on yon soft sunny steep,
As blows the wind, appears now green, now white :
Nature in it does still recruit and keep
The verdure, lacked by other trees in sight.

The birds of passage have, across the deep,
Already taken, by no easy flight,
Their weary broods, and shown them on the way
Nereids and Tritons and such beasts as they.

The Night has fought for empire and has won,
And captive leads away the shorter Day.
In the pure sky where fires eternal run,
Her starry chariot gaily goes its way;
Nor did it rise until the golden sun,
That other car, in Ocean's bosom lay.
The cold Orion shows his dagger then,
If Phœbus show his radiant face to men.

With this bright car of Night there goes along
A train of vigils, wakes, and anxious cares;
And Sleep, which (though he may be very strong)
When matched with these importunates, ill fares;
And pleasant dreams, which make the mind see wrong:
When it a weight of evil fortune bears.
Of health and wealth that man doth take his fill,
Who when he wakes is oft both poor and ill.

Oh wretched he who in so long a night
Can find no sleep and for the dawn doth pray,
If in his breast be strong desire alight
For what is promised by the coming day!
And though he tries, with both his brows knit tight,
To drive away sad thoughts and keep the gay,
To while away the time; the night appears,
Awake or sleeping, full a hundred years.

Oh wretched he whom on the waters now,
So long a night o'ertakes, far from the shore !
The wind that blows against the sightless prow
Obstructs its way, and loud the billows roar ;
Aurora called with many a prayer and vow,
Doth with her ancient spouse but stay the more.
He sadly counts and keeps in anxious sight
The sluggish footsteps of the tardy night.

How different, nay, how quite opposed, a fate
Is that of lovers in the winter's chill,
Who find that night goes at too fast a rate,
While day is dark, and dull, and hard to fill !
Now when rough winter presses with full weight.
The birds whose feathers are quite recent still,
Have ceased to sing—I scarce know which to say,
Whether a cheerful or a doleful lay.

The screeching cranes, still distant, come in sight,
And print the sky with varied forms and fair :
The last, with outstretched neck directs its flight.
Where left the first a track in empty air ;
And when in sunny places they alight,
One batch doth sleep, and one stands sentry there ;
A thousand birds, of every hue and sort,
Now fill the meads and on the waters sport.

Often the eagle, slowly circling round,
Doth threaten all, and flies above the mere :
All rise at once, and with the wind-like sound
Of wings they scare it.   But if, in the rear.
One of the feathered throng alone he found,
'Tis pounced on by the bird of Jove still near.

The wretched thing will much mistaken prove,
That thinks to go like Ganymede to Jove.

Zephyr has fled to Cyprus, where he plays
With flowers idly on the merry lawn;
The air, serene no more with golden haze,
By Aquilo and Boreas is torn;
The running, babbling rivulet now stays,
Confined by ice, and silent rests and worn;
The fish within the crystal hard and clear,
Like gnats in golden amber locked appear.

The hill[1] which makes fierce Caurus pass aside,
Lest he should hurt the beauteous flower, reared
Within its lap in honour, wealth, and pride,
Does now with mists its hoary head begird.
The snow already doth its shoulders hide,
Which from the proud head slope; the horrid beard
Now stiff with ice on the rough breast one sees;
The nose and eyes pour streams which heaven doth freeze.

The cloudy garland which encircles now
His lofty brow, is placed by Notus[2] there;
But Boreas coming from the Alps, doth blow
It off, and leaves the old head white and bare.
Again to clothe it Notus is not slow,
With mists which damp, malignant pinions bear.
Thus, bare or laden, for the plain below,
Angry Morello bodes now rain, now snow.

---

[1] Monte Morello, in whose lap Florence (*the beauteous flower*) may be said to lie. *Caurus* is the north-west wind.

[2] *Notus* is the south-west wind; *Boreas* is the north wind.

Of Æthiopia Auster[1] leave has ta'en,
All hot and dark, and thirsty sponges wets,
In the salt wave of the Tyrrhenian main.
Scarce to the destined coasts all tired he gets,
Begirt with clouds and heavy with the rain :
To squeezing both his fists at once he sets.
The happy streams, to meet the streams they know,
Then from the depths of ancient caverns flow.

They praise their father Ocean : wreathed around
Their brows are lilies now and river green ;
Their shells and twisted horns they loudly sound,
While, filled with pride, their flanks are swelling seen.
Their wrath conceived since many days has found
An object in the banks of timid mien.
Each foaming stream has its embankments burst,
Nor keeps the margin that it knew at first.

No more by crooked ways or paths oblique
They go like snakes ; but in great volumes bear
Onwards, and their primeval father seek.
United flow the streams that distant were,
And with each other, like old friends, they speak
About their countries and men's habits there ;
And talking thus in strange and altered strain,
Seek the lost outlet, but they seek in vain.

When, wide and swelled, the stream is stopped before
A narrow valley's lofty mountain-steeps,
The turbid waves, pent up, malignant roar ;
The flood is yellow with the earth it sweeps

---

[1] The south or south-west wind.

Stone upon stone against th' opposing shore,
On either hand, the angry river heaps.
It whirls and foams and shudders as it nears;
High out of reach, the shepherd sees and fears.

Thus, in its wrath the mighty flood doth spend
Its strength and fierce the adverse banks doth gnaw;
But in the plain, where it can wide extend,
As if appeased, 'tis almost heard no more.
As if in doubt to turn or to descend,
The distant hills have now become its shore.
The placid lake it proudly enters now,
With mountain spoils of many a trunk and bough.

The frightened goodwife scarce has time to throw
Open the sheds and set the cattle free.
She bears the cradle with her infant now,
Her grown-up daughter follows her, and see
'Neath clothes and sheets and wool her shoulders bow,
While all the cottage chattels floating be.
The pigs, the oxen, swim in fear and pain;
The sheep, I trow, will ne'er be shorn again.

Some of the household having safety sought
Up in the house-top, on the roof appear,
But see their little riches, dearly bought,
Their toil, their hope, submerged.　　But in their fear
For self, make no lament, nor utter ought.
The heart fears death within each bosom drear,
Nor seems to value what it dearest held;
The greater care has lesser care expelled.

The green familiar banks no more restrain
The happy fish who now have ampler space ;
Their old and natural wish they now obtain,
And see new shores : they go from place to place,
Led by this novel pleasure, nor refrain
From peeping at the wrecked and ruined face
Of walls and buildings which the waters fill ;
They like to see them, though uneasy still.

ALEXIS AND DORA.

(From Goethe, in the metre of the original.)

Ah! how unceasingly toils the ship, as she gets, every moment,
  Over the white-crested waves, further and further to sea!
Far away stretches the wake of the keel, and in it the dolphins
  Leap as they follow us close, seeming a prey to pursue.
All seems to augur a prosperous voyage; the mariner, tranquil,
  Gently is shifting the sail, doing its work for us all.
Forward the voyagers' mind, like the flags and the pennants, is tending:
  One alone, there by the mast, stands and looks sadly astern.
Blue are the mountains already; he sees them departing and sinking
  Into the sea; and with *them*, sinking all joy he sees.
Now too, O Dora! for thee has the ship which bears off thy Alexis,
  Even thy friend, thy betrothed, vanished in distance away.
Thou, too, art looking towards me in vain. Our hearts are still beating
  One for the other, but ah! next to each other no more.
Single moment in which I have lived! By thyself thou outweighest
  All the days which, before, coldly passed by without trace.
Ah! in that moment, the last one, in *thee* descended upon me,
  All unsuspected, a life sent by the Gods from above.
Vainly at present thy light, O Phœbus! illumines the ether;
  Hateful thy all-radiant day now has become unto me.

Let me turn inwards my thoughts, and look back; and in silence the
    period,
When I beheld her each day, let me go over again.
Who could such beauty have seen, and not have experienced its power?
Blunted indeed was thy soul if it was dead to such charms.
Blame not thyself, poor youth!—'Twas as when the Poet a riddle,
    Carefully guarded by words, unto his hearers propounds.
All with the pictures are pleased, and their graceful and rare com-
    bination;
Only the word is not there, giving the purport and sense.
When 'tis discovered at last, the cloud from all minds it dispelleth,
    Making the poem complete, doubling the charm of the whole.
Wherefore, O love! with such tardiness, didst thou unfasten the
    bandage
Which thou hadst bound o'er my eyes? Why didst thou lift it too
    late?
Long had the ship, ready freighted, been waiting for favouring breezes,
    When from the shore to the sea tended those breezes at last.
Empty times of my youth, and empty dreams of the future!
    Ye disappear from the scene; nought but that hour remains.
Yes, it remains; the joy remains; I hold thee, O Dora!
    Hope in his mirror displays, Dora, thy image alone.
Often I saw thee repair to the temple, adorned and yet modest;
    Also thy mother I saw; gravely she went by thy side.
Eager thou wast and alert, in bearing the produce to market;
    Ay, and how bravely thy head balanced the urn from the fount!
Visible then was thy throat and exposed was thy neck unto all
    men;
All could the measure admire, which to thy movements belongs.
Often in fear I looked on, and thought that the pitcher was slipping:
    Firmly it stood on the cloth, twisted in circular shape.
Beautiful neighbour mine! I thus was accustomed to see thee,
    As we look up to the stars, or as we gaze at the moon:

Pleasure we feel at their sight, but never the faintest desire
    That they should be our own findeth a place in the heart.
Years, it was thus that ye passed : not twenty paces the houses
    Stood from each other; and yet never her threshold I touched.
Now by the sea we are parted.   O wave! thou but apest the heaven
    Even thy glorious blue seems but the colour of night.
All were already astir, when a boy came suddenly running
    Up to my father's abode, calling me down to the beach.
Rising the sail is already, he cried ; in the wind it is flapping ;
    Ay, and the anchor, upheaved, mightily cleaveth the sand.
Come Alexis, oh come!—and my excellent father then laying
    Gravely his hand on my head, gave me the blessing I asked.
Full of kind forethought, my mother then brought an additional bundle.
    When thou returnest, they cried, mayst thou be happy and rich !
And so I hurried away with the bundle under my shoulder,
    Down by the wall ; and behold, there thou wast, close to the gate
Of thy garden.   Thou smiledst upon me, and saidest, Alexis,
    Is't with that noisy crew thou art about to embark ?
Foreign shores thou art going to visit, to buy for the wealthy
    Matrons here of the town, fabrics and ornaments rare ;
Wilt thou not also buy me a neck-chain, a small one ? most gladly
    Will I repay thee the price ; oft such a trinket I've wished !
Stopping, by thee thus addressed, I asked thee as asketh a merchant,
    Details exact of the chain, as to its shape and its weight.
Modest indeed was the price which thou bargain'dst, and I, as thou
        spokest,
    Fastened my eyes on thy neck, worthy the gems of a queen.
Louder the shouting became from the ship ; but thou saidest, all
        friendly,
    Now, from this garden of mine, with thee some fruit thou must
        take ;
Take of the oranges, only the ripest ; of figs, but the white ones ;
    Fruit is unknown to the sea ; nor in all lands is there such.

So I went in; and thou busily pluckedst the fruit, and the golden
    Load in thy skirt was received, stretching the folds thou hadst
    raised.
Oft I entreated and cried 'twas enough; but ever some richer
    Fruit from the branches above, fell, scarcely touched, in thy hand.
Up to a bower thou camest at last, and a basket we found there;
    Thick was the myrtle that hung, flowery, o'er our heads.
Silently then, and with skill, the fruit to arrange thou begannest:
    First was the orange put in, ponderous like a gold ball;
Next came the delicate fig, which the slightest of pressures disfigures;
    Myrtle was placed on the top, beauty to add to the gift.
Ay, but I took it not up; I stood still; and we looked at each other.
    Full in the eyes for a while; dim then my vision became.
Bosom on bosom reposed; and now with my hand I encircled,
    Softly the beautiful neck, cov'ring with kisses the throat;
Thy head sank on my shoulder; now also thy arms, in their sweet-
    ness,
    Gently around me were thrown; I was the happiest of men.
Love's strong hands I felt; he forcibly pressed us together.
    Thrice, in the sky without cloud, thunder I heard. And the tears
Flowed more than once from my eyes; thou weptest; I wept; and
    that moment,
    Full both of grief and of bliss, seemed like the end of the world.
Louder and louder the shouts on the beach, my feet would not bear
    me,
    Though I endeavoured; I cried: Dora, and art thou not mine?
Yes, and for ever! thou murmur'dst, and lo, the tears we were
    shedding,
    Seemed of a sudden dispelled, as by the breath of a god.
Nearer a cry of "Alexis!" was heard; and the boy who sought me
    Showed us his face at the gate. Gladly the basket he took.
Oh, how he urged me to haste! I pressed thy hand; but I know not
    How I got into the ship, for I inebriate seemed;

Ay, and my comrades thought so, or thought I was ill, and they
 spared me.
Then in dim distance and mist, soon did the town disappear.
" Ever," thou murmur'dst, O Dora! the word in my ears is still ring-
 ing,
Mixed with the thunder of Zeus, near to whose heavenly throne
Stood his daughter the Goddess of Love, and beside her the Graces;
 Is not the union I ask, ratified thus by the Gods?
Oh, then hasten, thou ship, with all the favouring breezes!
 Toil, ye powerful bows, cleaving the white-crested waves!
Bear me across to the foreign seaport, so that the goldsmith
 May in the workshop at once fashion the heavenly pledge.
Verily, into a chain thy chainlet shall turn, O my Dora!
 Nine times loosely entwined shall it encircle thy neck.
Other ornaments, too: I will get the most various; and golden
 Bracelets as well thou shalt have, richly thy hand to adorn.
There shall the ruby the emerald rival; the sapphire sweetly
 Next to the jacinth be placed, while by the setting of gold,
Fast shall the jewels be held, in rich combination, together.
 Ne'er shall the bride be adorned, save by the bridegroom alone!
If I should look upon pearls, of thee I shall think, and thy lovely
 Tapering hand I shall see, if I should look on a ring.
Yes, I will barter and buy; thou shalt choose of the best and the
 finest;
 All that the cargo makes up, would thou couldst take to thyself!
Yet not ornaments only and gems will thy lover procure thee:
All that a housewife delights, that will I get for thee too:
Delicate blankets of wool, adorned with edges of purple,
 Such as will make us a bed, warm and cosy and soft;
Pieces of beautiful linen. Thou sittest and sewest and clothest
 Me and thyself, and, I hope, even a third one besides.
Pictures of hope, oh delude me! Ye Deities, lessen the fire
 Which in my bosom is lit, raging each moment more fierce.

Ah! but how oft I regret it, that pain that with pleasure was mingled,
  When I perceive the approach, frigid, familiar, of Care!
No, not the torch of the Furies, or yell of the hell-hounds, can startle,
  In the abodes of Despair, him who is conscious of guilt,
More than the spectre appalled me,—the spectre which coolly the fair
  one
  Let me behold from afar. Open the garden gate stands;
Ay, but another goes in; for *him*, too, the fruit is collected;
  Also the fig unto *him* yieldeth its nourishing juice;
Up to the bower enticed, does he enter? Ye Deities blind me!
  Ay, and that picture of joy quick from my memory wipe!
Yes! a maiden she is; and she who so hurriedly giveth
  Herself up to the one, quick to the other will turn.
Laugh not this time, O Zeus, at the oaths with such insolence broken!
  Thunder more terribly! Strike! . . . No, thy dread lightning
  retain;
After me send the uncertain clouds; in the darkness nocturnal,
  Let thy most dazzling of bolts strike this unfortunate mast!
Scatter the planks and the spars; give these goods to be tossed by the
  waters;
  And to the dolphins, O Zeus, let me be given for food!
Now, ye Muses, enough: in vain ye endeavour to picture
  How, in the bosom that loves, fluctuate joy and pain:
Heal ye cannot, indeed, the wounds that by Love are inflicted;—
  No; but the balm that shall soothe, ye in your kindness can pour.

AMYNTAS.

(*From Goethe.*)

Nicias, kindest of men, of body and soul the physician,
  Ailing I am, in good sooth; ah, but thy remedy's hard!
Fortitude melted away when I wanted to follow thy counsel;
  Yes, and the truest of friends, seems in my eyes like a foe.
Think not I seek to refute; to myself I say all that thou urgest;
  Even the bitterer word, which thou withholdest, as well.
Ah! but the water comes pouring down from the clefts of the moun-
        tains
  Fast; and the waves of the stream, who can detain them with songs?
Rages the storm not unceasingly? Doth not the sun in the evening
  Roll from the zenith of Day into the depths of the sea?
Yes, and all Nature proclaims it, and says to me: "Thou too, Amyntas,
  To irresistible laws, framed by stern powers, must yield."
Frown not still deeper, my Friend; but hear, I entreat thee, with
        patience,
  What I was taught by a tree, yesterday near to the brook.
Few are the apples it gives me, this tree once so heavily laden:
  See, 'tis the ivy in fault, clinging around it with force.
And I seized my knife, my sickle-shaped knife, which is sharpest;
  Severed and cut with it deep, tearing down wreath upon wreath.

Ay, but I started with fear; for a voice deep-sighing and plaintive,
   Seeming to come from the boughs, murmured close by me these
     words:
Oh, do not injure me thus, thy faithful garden companion,
   Who when thou wast but a lad, gave thee enjoyment oft!
Oh, do not injure me thus! thou art tearing away with this network,
   Which thou so roughly destroy'st, that which is part of my life.
Have I not fed it myself, and tenderly nurtured and reared it?
   Is not its foliage, oh say, part of myself, like my own?
Shall I not love it, this plant, which has need of myself and no other,
   Which with a covetous force, round me has silently wound?
Thousands of tendrils have rooted; and thousands on thousands of
     fibres
Fastened their hold and sank in, searching the depths of my life.
Food it deriveth from me, enjoying that which I needed,
   Sucking the marrow away, draining the essence of life.
Vainly I nourishment take; the powerful root can send upwards,
   Striving to quicken the tree, only one half of the sap.
Now that the dangerous guest, albeit adored, intercepteth,
   E'en as it mounteth, the force needed in autumn for fruit,
Nothing can reach to the summit; the shoots and extremities wither:
   Even the branch o'er the stream now has to wither begun.
Yes, 'tis the traitress's fault; she cheats me of life and of riches,
   Cheats me of courage and strength; cheats me of prospects and
     hope.
Feeling I have but for her who encircles me; loving my fetters,
   Loving the ornament dire, formed of extraneous green.
Use not therefore thy knife, O Nicias! but spare the unhappy
   Wretch who his bondage enjoys, slowly consumed by his love.
Every expenditure's sweet: oh let me the fairest enjoy!
   Who that to love has recourse setteth a value on life?

EPIGRAM FROM GOETHE.

OFTEN were urn and sarcophagus circled with life by the Pagan :
Fauns are seen dancing around, with the bacchantes in troop,
Forming a motley array; while gaily the goat-footed Satyr
Forces the hoarsest of tones out of the echoing horn,
Cymbals and timbrels resound; we look at the marble and hear it ;
Then there are fluttering birds; sweet are the berries they peck.
Little the din do they mind; and still less does it frighten the
    Cupid,
Who, in the midst of the throng, carries triumphant his torch.
Death is thus crushed by luxuriance; the ashes which here are
    reposing
Seem, in their silent abode, still to get pleasure from life.

FROM GOETHE'S *WILHELM MEISTER*.

He who with tears ne'er ate his bread,
Who through night's miserable hours
Ne'er weeping sat upon his bed,
He knows you not, ye heavenly Powers.

Ye first the wretch with life endowed :
That he should sin ye then permitted ;
And then his torture ye allowed :
For ne'er was wrong on earth remitted.

THE LIMITS OF HUMANITY.

(From Goethe.)

When the primeval
Holiest Father
With easy hands scatters,
From clouds that are rolling,
Lightnings like blessings
O'er the earth broadcast :
I then kiss the lowest
Hem of his garment,
With faith and a childlike
Awe in my heart.

With the Gods never
Let any mortal
Measure his strength :
If he soars upwards
Till his head touches
Even the stars,
The soles of his feet, then,
Uncertain rest nowhere ;
The sport he becometh
Of clouds and of winds.

If he stands solidly
On his feet planted,
On the immovable
Durable earth,
Then doth his stature
Rival not even
That of the oak-tree
Or of the vine.

How do Gods differ
From human beings?
Thus: in *their* presence
Many waves hasten,
Stream without end;
Us the wave tosses,
Us the wave swallows,
In it we sink.

A tiny ring
Contains our lifetime;
And our generations,
Unnumbered, are gathered
Round the unlimited
Chain of *their* life.

TO ITALY.

(From the Italian of Leopardi, in the original metre.)

O NATIVE land, I see the wall, the arch,
The column and the statue, and our lone
Ancestral towers still there;
But glory I see *not*,
The steel and laurel under which did march
Our sires of old.   Disarmed, thou long hast shown
A naked forehead and a bosom bare.
Woe's me! what wounds be they!
What pallor and what gore!   In what a state
Art thou, woman most beautiful!   I call
On Earth and Heaven: say,
Oh say, who did all this? and worse her fate;
For both her arms are bound with heavy chains;
She sits unveiled, with locks that loosened fall,
On the bare ground, abandoned and forlorn,
While hid her face remains
Between her knees, and weeps.
Weep on, for well thou mayst, my Italy,
That to excel was born, not less in woe than in prosperity.

If thy two eyes were now two living founts,
Ne'er would their weeping be
Sufficient for thy evil and the shame.
That art a slave that wast a queen of yore.
Who thy famed past recounts
In speech or writing, and says not of thee:
"She once was great, but now is great no more"?
Oh why, oh why? where is the ancient strength,
The arms, the courage, the endurance, where?
Who took thy falchion bright?
Who first betrayed? What arts, oh say at length,
What force was brought to bear,
To strip thee of thy mantle and thy crown?
How, from so great a height,
Didst thou descend to such a depth of shame?
Hast thou no champion? What, none of thy own
Defend thy cause? Arms! arms! for I alone
For thee will fight and fall, without the rest.
Grant that my blood as flame
May be, O Heaven, for each Italic breast!

Where are thy sons? I hear a sound of arms,
Of chariots and of shouting, and a clash
Of cymbals: thy sons fight
In distant foreign lands.
Attend, O Italy! attend! for swarms
I seem to see, of horse and foot, that dash
'Mid smoke and dust, and swords that flash in sight,
Like lightnings through a mist.
Dost thou not hope? and on the doubtful odds
Dost thou not fear to fix thy trembling eyes?
Why in yon fight insist
The youths of Italy? O Gods! O Gods!

Italian swords fight for another land.
Oh woe to him who in the battle dies,
Not for his children dear, his faithful wife,
Nor for his fathers' strand,
But slain by others' foes,
For other men, and dying, cannot say :
"Dear native land, the life
Which thou didst give, I give thee back this day."

Oh, brave those ancient times, and dear and blest,
When men were wont to rush
To death in squadrons for their native land ;
And ye Thessalian Straits, for ever great
And honoured, which attest
How a few brave and generous souls could crush
The strength of Persia and the strength of Fate.
Methinks the plants, the water, and the stones,
And your high crags, the passing stranger tell,
With accents indistinct,
How the whole place was covered with the bones
Of serried ranks that fell,
But all unconquered, in the cause of Greece ;
How Xerxes' name was linked
To endless shame, and with a coward's wrath
He fled across the Hellespont for peace ;
While from Antela's steep, where death had made
A life eternal for the sacred band,
Simonides looked forth
Upon the sky, upon the sea and land.

And with his cheeks still moistened with his tears,
With heaving chest, with faltering steps undone,
He seized his sounding lyre :

" Oh three times blest are you
Whose breasts were offered to the hostile spears
For love of her who gave you to the Sun !
Ye whom Greece honours and mankind admires !
What drove you into arms ?
What mighty love o'er your young hearts had power ?
What love impelled you to the bitter chance ?
Oh say, ye youths, what charms
Did ye discover in that parting hour,
That ye should court a hard and mournful fate ?
'Twas not to death ye went, but to some dance,
'Twas some rare feast ye were in haste to reach.
But Tartarus did wait
You, and the stagnant pools ;
Nor were your wives, your children by your side,
Upon this rugged beach,
Where all unkissed and all unwept ye died.

But not without the Persians' hard defeat,
And endless woe and shame.
As bounds a lion 'mid a herd of bulls,
And leaps on this and that, and in his back
Lets teeth resistless meet,
And now a thigh, and now a flank doth maim ;
So raged the fury of the Greek attack
Amid the masses of the Persian host.
See horse and rider intermingled lie !
See how the flying throng
By cars are hampered and by tents o'ertossed !
See 'mid the first that fly
The pallid tyrant with dishevelled hair !
See the Greek heroes strong—
Whose limbs, red with barbaric blood, attest

What boundless loss the Persians have to bear—
Little by little, conquered by their wounds,
Fall in a gory heap !   Oh hail, oh hail
To you, the three times blest,
So long as men shall tell, or write, the tale !

The loosened stars shall into ocean fall,
And hissing perish in the depths below,
Before your fame be past,
Or love for you be less.
Your graves are altars ; and the mothers all
Shall bring their sons, and of your blood shall show
The noble vestiges.   Behold, I cast
Me down, ye blessed souls ;
And now these rocks, and now these clods I kiss,
Which shall be praised and ever famous now
To Earth's remotest poles.
Would I could rest beside you, and that this
Dear earth with my own heart's blood could be wet !
But if the Fates are adverse, nor allow
That I for Greece my parting breath should give
Upon the field, oh let
At least the Gods permit
That, in far times to come, your poet's name,
Modest though 'tis, may live,
And live as long as shall have lived your fame."

LOVE AND DEATH.[1]

(*From the Italian of Leopardi.*)

"Ὃν οἱ θεοὶ φιλοῦσιν ἀποθνήσκει νέος.—*Menander*.

BROTHER and Sister, Love and Death, did Fate
In the same hour create.
Two other things so fair
Be not on earth, nor in the realms of air.
The one to greatest good
And greatest bliss gives birth
That in the ocean of existence lies :
The other upon earth
Annuls all ills that be.
A beauteous maiden she,
Whose form delights the eye ;
Not such as cowards fancy her, but oft
The stripling Love's adored
Companion fair and soft.

---

[1] Throughout the whole of this poem, the reader must bear in mind that in Italian, as in the other languages of Latin origin, the word *Death* is feminine, and that Death itself therefore naturally appears to the Italian mind in the form of a female.

And thus together o'er men's paths they fly,
And to wise hearts the best of help afford;
For ne'er was heart more wise
Than when enamoured; or more fit to spurn
The ills decreed above;
Or for another Lord
Than Love, so ready dangers to incur:
For where thou art, O Love,
Lo, courage takes its rise
Or wakes again; and wise in act and deed,
Not in mere thought, as they were oft ere then,
Become the sons of men.

Whenever, in the deep
Recesses of the heart,
Love's touch is first impressed,
We feel, together with it, in the breast
A languid wish for Death's eternal sleep.
Why, I know not; but such
Of strong true love is the most certain test.
Perhaps these desert shores
Then first appal the sight; perhaps the earth,
Whose face has uninhabitable grown,
Man now surveys and seeks
In vain the new and sole
And boundless bliss to which his thought now soars
But feeling something in his heart which speaks
Of coming storms, encountered for that bliss,
He yearns to reach a port,
Pressed by the fierce desire
Which round him roars and darker darker grows.

And when the dreaded Power

Envelops all around,
And Care unconquered thunders in the heart,
How often then, O Death,
With yearning most intense,
Upon thy help the suff'ring lover calls !
How oft when twilight falls,
Or when, at dawn, he sink at last to sleep
With weary limbs, he wishes that he ne'er
May rise again to weep,
And ne'er behold the bitter light again !
Oft at the echo of a dying knell,
Or dirge with which are ta'en
Away the dead to their eternal rest,
He draweth ardent sighs
Deep from the breast, and envies him who now
Is on his way with the extinct to lie.
E'en the neglected poor,
The village churl, who knows
None of the virtues which the schools imply,
Even the little peasant maiden shy,
Whose hair would stand upright
If Death were named, from fright,
Now nerved by Constancy, have strength to meet
With steady eye the trappings of the grave ;
Have strength to brood, and brave
The poison or the steel,
And learn full well to feel,
In their untutored mind, that Death is sweet.

So much Love's discipline
Inclineth us to Death. Full many a time,
When the great inner strife has reached such pitch,
That to support it mortal strength must fail,

The body, all too frail,
Yields to the frightful shocks, and in this way
Death doth through the fraternal power prevail;
Or Love so goadeth to the dark abyss,
That of their own accord the school-less churl
And maiden weak uplift a violent hand,
And lay their youthful limbs low in the dust.
The world derides all this,
And lives to good old age at Heaven's command.

To all who happy are,
Or ardent, or are brave,
May Fate let one or other of you come,
Ye gentle Powers, by far
The kindest friends of man,
Unto whose sway there is no sway that can
Be matched in the great universe, save one,
The all-surpassing power of Fate alone.
And thou, whose name, e'en from my earliest years
All honoured, I invoke,
Fair Death, that art on earth
Alone compassionate of earthly tears:
If e'er thy name divine
I praised, or made thee some amends when loud
The vulgar thankless crowd
Did wrong thee and malign,—
Delay no more, yield now
To unfamiliar prayer;
Close these sad eyelids mine
To Heaven's light, O Queen of Ages thou!

And thou wilt find me, when thou shalt expand
Thy wings at my entreaty, standing there

Armed and with head unbowed,
Resisting Fate uncowed;
Not heaping praises on the cruel hand
Which scourges and is dyed
Red in my guiltless blood,
Nor blessing it, as man
Has done for ages from a coward's mood.
Each childish hope, with which mankind console
Themselves, each solace vain,
Thou shalt behold me cast
Away in scorn; at all times making thee
My hope, my comfort sole;
Deeming but that day blest
When I shall lay my face in sleep at last
Upon thy virgin breast.

CONSALVO.

(From Leopardi.)

NEAR to the term of his abode on earth
Consalvo lay ; rebellious for a while
Against his fate ; but now no more ; for scarce
Midway in his fifth lustre, o'er his head
Hung the implored oblivion.   There he lay,
As he for long had lain, on this last day,
Abandoned by the friends he most had loved ;
For in the long-run not a friend on earth
Remains to him who holds from earth aloof.
Yet by his side there stood, by pity led
To comfort him in his deserted state,
She, who, alone and ever, filled his thoughts,
Elvira, famed for loveliness divine ;
Who knew her power, and who knew that one
Of her bright looks, or word in kindness said,
Rehearsed a thousand and a thousand times
By his tenacious thought, was wont to be
For her unhappy lover help and food :
Although she ne'er had heard a word of love
Drop from his lips.   For always in his soul

Excess of fear had yet more potent proved
Than strong desire; so that he had become,
Through too much love, a very slave and child.

But death at last the bond of silence broke,
So long endured : for feeling that the signs
Of coming dissolution were too clear,
He took her hand as she was leaving him,
And pressing that white hand within his own,
Said : "Thou art leaving, by the hour warned :
Farewell, Elvira. Ne'er again, I think,
Shall I behold thee. So farewell. I give
Thee, for thy care, more thanks than with my lips
I can express. And surely a reward
Thou wilt obtain, if Heaven rewards the good."
Pale turned the fair one as she heard these words,
And held her breath ; because the human heart,
Even the stranger's heart, is quick to sink
When one who is departing on his ways
Doth bid farewell for ever. To gainsay
The dying youth she sought, and from him hide
His fate's approach. But interrupting her,
He thus continued : " Welcome is the death
Which now descends upon me, and thou know'st
How oft implored. I fear it not; and this
My final day seems happy. But I grieve
To part from thee for ever. Yes, alas !
I leave thee now for ever; and my heart
Breaks at the thought. Ne'er more to see thy eyes
Or hear thy voice ! But tell me : ere thou leave
Me for all time, wilt thou, Elvira, not
Bestow on me a kiss ?—one single kiss,
In all my life ! Unto a dying man

A boon is ne'er refused. Thou needst not fear
Lest of the gift I boast, I, almost dead,
Whose lips a stranger's hand to-day will soon
For ever close." And having said these words,
He, in entreaty, laid his chilly lips,
With a deep sigh, upon the hand beloved.

The lovely woman undecided stood,
And thoughtful; and she fixed her eyes, in which
A thousand beauties sparkled, upon those
Of the unhappy youth, in which the last
Bright tear-drop shone. She could not find the heart
To spurn his prayer, and by refusal make
His sad farewell more bitter; but was seized
With pity for the love she knew so well.
She laid her heavenly face, she laid those lips,
So much desired, and which had been for years
The subject of his dreams and of his sighs,
Gently upon the sufferer's face, which now
Already wore the pallid hue of death,
And kiss on kiss, with tenderness intense
And deepest pity, on the quivering lips
Of her enraptured trembling lover, pressed.

What change came o'er thee then? What aspect new
Did life and death and woe assume for thee,
Consalvo, fleeting fast? Pressing her hand,
His loved Elvira's hand, which still he held
Against his heart, which with the latest throb
Of death and love was beating, "Oh," he cried,
"Elvira, my Elvira, surely still
I am on earth; those lips were surely thine,
And 'tis thy hand which lies within my own!
It seems a soul's first vision, or a dream

Or miracle. Elvira, ah how much,
How much I owe to death! The love I felt
Was never kept a secret from thyself
Or others, for true love on earth is ne'er
To be concealed. 'Twas manifest enough
In every act; the haggard face, the eyes,
All spoke, save words. Now and for evermore
The boundless passion which usurps my heart
Would still be mute, unless that heart had been
Made bold by Death's approach. I now shall die
Content with fate, and mourn no more the day
When first I saw the light. Not vain my life,
Since it was granted that upon those lips
My lips should press. Nay, I esteem my lot
A happy one. The world hath two fair things
Called Love and Death: Heaven leads me to the one
While in the bloom of youth; the other makes
Me fortunate indeed. Ah, if but once,
Ay, only once, thou hadst appeased and soothed
My pent-up love, the earth would have become
For evermore a very Paradise .
In my all-altered eyes! Old age itself,
Abhorred old age, I should have then endured
With tranquil heart; the memory alone
Of that one instant would have been enough
For one who could repeat: 'I once was blest
As none was ever blest.' But ah, such bliss
Is not conceded by the powers above
To earthly nature! Such a love as this
Is not allied to joy. And, as its price,
Into tormentors' hands, ay, to the scourge,
The wheel, the stake, I would have gladly flown
From out thy arms; I would have hurried down
To the dread realm of everlasting woe.

" Elvira, O Elvira, happy he,
Above immortals happy, on whom thou
Dost smile the smile of love !   And happy next
Is he who gives his blood and life for thee !
Yes, yes, 'tis granted (and it is no dream,
As I long thought), 'tis granted here on earth
To reach to bliss.   I knew it on the day
When first I watched thee.   But 'twas for my death
That I so did.   But yet not even once,
Despite such anguish, had I strength to curse
That cruel day with certainty of heart.

" And thou, live happy, and adorn the world,
Elvira, with thy presence.   None will e'er
Love thee as I have loved thee; such a love
May not again have birth.   How oft, how oft
By poor Consalvo, in that weary time,
Wast thou invoked and mourned for and bewept !
How, at Elvira's name, my heart has sunk,
My cheek turned pale; how I have trembling stood
Upon thy bitter threshold, at the sound
Of that angelic voice, or sight of that
Fair brow, I, who now tremble not at death!
Farewell, Elvira.   With the vital spark
Thy cherished image now at length departs
From out my heart.   Farewell.   But if my love
Was not too irksome, then to-morrow come,
And by my bier at nightfall heave a sigh."

He ceased ; nor was it long ere with his voice
His spirit fled ; and ere the set of sun
His first fair day had vanished from his sight.

TO HIMSELF.

(From Leopardi.)

Now thou'lt for ever rest,
My weary heart. The last delusion's dead :
My own eternity. 'Tis dead. I feel
For day-dreams cherished once
Not the mere hope, the very wish extinct.
For ever rest. Enough
Thou now hast throbbed. Thy motions are worth nought.
Nor is the earth deserving of a sigh.
Bitter and dull is life,
Never aught else ; the world is only mire.
Subside at length. Despair
For the last time. For human kind had Fate
No gift but death. And now despise thyself,
And Nature, and the cruel
Power which, hidden, rules for general woe ;
And the unbounded vanity of all.

TO THE MOON.

(*From Leopardi.*)

O BEAUTEOUS Moon, I call to mind that here,
A year ago, upon this same hillside,
I came, with anguish filled, to look on thee,
And thou wast poiséd over yonder wood,
Just like to-day, and filling it with light.
But tremulous and misty through the tears
Which on my lashes hung, before my eyes
Thou didst appear; for bitter was my life;
And 'tis so still.   It changeth not its ways,
O my belovéd Moon.   But yet I love
To think it o'er, and to note down the age
Of my own grief.   And oh how sweet it is
In this our time of youth, when still the flight
Of hope is long, and that of mem'ry short,
To let the thoughts revert to things gone by,
Though sad they be, and though the woe endures!

THE EVENING OF THE HOLIDAY.

(From Leopardi.)

SOFT is the night, and clear and without wind,
And placid o'er the roofs and gardens rests
The moon, which from a distance lighteth up
Serene each mountain-side. O my beloved,
Each lane is silent now; the midnight lamp
Through balconies shines softly here and there!
Thou slumb'rest, for an easy sleep has sought
Thee in thy quiet rooms; and nought like care
Is guarding thee, nor dost thou think or guess
How deep a wound thou in my breast hast struck.
Thou art asleep: I at the window stand,
And hail the sky that wears so mild a face,
And Nature ancient and omnipotent,
Who made me but for woe : "To thee be hope
Denied," she said; "ay, even hope, and let
Nought ever sparkle in thy eyes but tears."
This day has been eventful, and thou now
Dost rest from pleasure, and dost dream, perchance,
Of all the many thou to-day hast pleased,
And who pleased thee. Not I am in thy thoughts,

Nor ever hoped to be.   Meanwhile I ask
How long I yet shall live, and on the ground
I lie and cry and rage.   O frightful days!
And youth so green!   But hark, upon the road,
I hear, near by, a solitary song:
Some artisan who late at night returns
After his revels to his humble home.
I feel a cruel tightening of the heart
E'en as I think how all on earth goes by
And scarcely leaves a trace.   And now has fled
The festive day; and after it there comes
The common day; and so Time sweeps away
Each human incident.   Where is the hum
Of all those ancient peoples? where the cry
Of all our glorious ancestors, and where
The sway of that great Rome whose clash of arms
Went forth upon the lands and oceans once?
All now is peace and silence, and the world
Is in repose, and all is now forgot.
E'en in my earliest years, the years in which
A holiday with longing we await,
I, when the day was over, lay in bed,
In pain and sleepless; and, deep in the night,
A song that reached me from the lanes outside,
And in the distance slowly died away,
Struck a like pang already to my heart.

THREE FRAGMENTS FROM ALEARDI.

I.

(From the opening of the 'Sette Soldati.')

This is the valley: I behold it black
And uniform: a pass
Deserted, which two mountain-backs enclose
Abruptly, and which ne'er
The roses of the dawn or sunset knows.
A stream its bottom furrows; kites and mists
Furrow the air.   Of smoke a light-blue streak
That curleth upwards from a human home
Ye long in vain might seek
Far as the eye can roam.

    .   .   .   .   .

. . . . A hidden subterranean fire
Once shook the place, and from the mountain-side
Were downward hurled the innumerable stones
Of monstrous size, which now before us loom
Erect and white, and look
Each like a giant's tomb.
With rapid foot the frightened goatherd flies
Who ventures here; for ever and anon

[1] See an article on the " Contemporary Italian Poets " in the
' Quarterly Review ' for October 1877.

Is heard the whistling sound
Caused by the livid fragments of basalt,
As down the slopes they bound;
And seeks with trembling prayer to reinforce
The symbol of the cross.
And from each height, when here a storm has passed,
Pours from a hundred shells,
In curved and fugitive
Cascades, the waters' sudden overgrowth;
On every side, the dells
Re-echo with the fall of many drops;
The vast extent of green
Is lighted up, and moving rainbows then
Fill the whole savage scene.

II.

(From 'Arnalda di Roca.')

    . . . . Moments there are,
At periods when the misery of life
Is at its height, when suddenly we seem
To see the darkness which the future hides
Illumined; and we seem to hear a voice,
Inward, mysterious, heard but by the heart,
Predicting that the cherished daily things
Which we around us see, and which by time
Have come to form a portion of ourselves,
We now behold for the last time on earth—
And so we seek and note them one by one;
And firmly print their image on the mind,
As if foreseeing that too soon will come
Still sadder days, in which, when far away,
We shall take bitter pleasure in their thought.

III.

THE BLOWING UP OF THE TURKISH GALLEYS.

(From ' Arnalda di Roca.')

Living and dead, oppressors and oppressed,
And the rapacious galleys, which had been
The scene of so much woe, all disappeared
Within the bosom of a fiery sea,
As in a sleep of terror disappears
A morbid dream.   The ripped-up billows fled
In foaming circles.   O'er a vast extent
Descended from the red and fiery skies,
And hissed and crackled on the waves, a rain
Of red-hot cinders and of human limbs
Dissevered, and of smoking bits of spar.

All passed away.   The stillness which precedes
The dawn is smiling on the lovely bay.
The bracing air is silent : and along
The mountain paths, the hedges tremulous
Of orange and of lavender give birth
To morning perfumes ; and attract the sweet
Wren and the joyous skylark, which now flies
Towards the sunrise.   And of all that life,
Distracted lately by a hate so deep,
Remains alone a solitary cloud
Of smoke, which licks the waters on the spot
Where stood the ships.   An eagle's cry is heard
As down it swoops upon its morning prey.
The surf is heard as on the shore it breaks,
And casts an oar or human head upon
The lonely sands.   No other sound disturbs
The boundless air; for Nature liveth on,
And a vain mist are human hates and loves.

FROM THE *CARNEVALE* OF CARDUCCI.

VOICE FROM THE PALAZZI.

WHETHER, O Borcas, thou
Be roaming through the echoing dale or wood
Of sounding pine, or moaning unreleased
Beneath dark cloisters, now
Uttering human wail, or sound that could
Come from a flute, or roar of wounded beast;
I love thee well.   And, lonely Winter, thee
With pleasure, too, on yonder Alps I see.

A whitish mist fills all
The sleeping air, and on the horizon wide
Blends with the plain, which now by snow is hid.
Pinkish and weak and small,
The solar disc seems in the haze to hide
Like to a human eye without its lid.
Among the plants no breath of wind, no bird;
No song of girl or wayfarer is heard.

Only the boughs, which creak,
Tired of the unequal burden which they bear,
Or the sharp sound when something frozen splits.
Ay, let Arcadia speak
Of Zephyr, and recall his kindred fair.
But I prefer these stern and silent fits
Of Nature.   Do, Eurilla, try and raise
From these dull embers a more cheerful blaze.

VOICE FROM THE HOVELS.

Oh if the living blood
From my own heart could but your warmth recall,
Ye limbs of this my child that icy lie!
But my heart's sluggish flood
Scarce moves, and rigid my embraces fall;
For man is deaf, and God above too high.
Oh lay thy tear-bathed face, thou poor weak
And helpless child, against thy mother's cheek.

Not on a mother's breast
Thy brother died; but slowly on the road
His parting gasps were stilled by the snow.
One day at eve, oppressed
With work, he followed 'neath a heavy load
His masters hard, with faltering steps and slow.
And earth and air conspired with man to wage
A war against him with relentless rage.

The drifting snow-flakes whipped
The exhausted boy through the thin rags he wore;
He fell, and bleeding rose, but all in vain;

For fast from hunger slipped
His strength away ; till on that pathway sore
He was o'ercome, and Death cut short his pain :
Then as a corpse, unshrouded and defaced,
Before his mother he once more was placed.

A FIRST OF NOVEMBER EVENING.[1]

(From the Italian of Arnaboldi.)

THE first November day already wanes.
In their slow journey downwards to the plain
Have come the herds, that autumn has expelled
From 'mong the hills ; and the monotonous
Low tinkle of the leader-heifer's bell
No more is heard.   In long extended line
Now almost all the birds have flown away
Who dread the winter's cold.   At most, are seen
Some tardy flights of larks, who high in air
Suspended, to more gentle climes direct
Their strength of wing ; and in a little while,
On top of oaks and walnut-trees, the crows
Will loudly caw.   Down through the valleys wide,
Through which is reached the higher range of Alps,
Blows a chill breeze, announcing unto all
In the Pre-Alpine tract, that the great woods
Of fir, and fragrant virgin pastures, now

---

[1] The eve of the day which, in Catholic countries, is devoted
to the memory of the dead.

L

Are white with snow. The sky's vast vault enwraps
Itself in clouds and mists; the lake is grey;
My own sweet Eupilis;[1] and other mists
Are rising from its surface; through their midst
A flight of wild-ducks passes rapidly.
In regiments or clumps upon the shores
Denuded now the poplar-trees rise up
Like melancholy ghosts; the chestnut-trees
Give back to earth their sere and yellow leaves
Upon my own hillside; whilst, at its foot,
The crops are pushing, unperceived as yet,
Their earliest shoots. And unto me, who sit
Here in my solitary room and read,
There comes the echo of a parting knell.

How many dyings by that bell are mourned!

A deep lament: to undiscovered shores,
All unillumined by a ray of sun,
Beyond the limits of both space and time,
It hurries us away. In it there is
A sadness and a yearning all unknown
To our most ancient fathers. Happy they,
Those earlier comers who ne'er let the course
Of placid thought push on beyond the flames
Of the funereal pyre! The world of myths
Then loved to run, through city, field, and wood,
In a perennial riot. Oh give me back
Radiant Olympus and its thousand Gods—
The Gods of gladness, the illustrious

---

[1] The classic name for the Lake of Pusiano, one of the smaller
lakes of the Milanese, already celebrated in Italian literature,
from its connection with Parini.

Sons of a Nature filled with endless life!
Who hath the power to give back again
Unto the world the time of wondrous youth,
When all was light and all ambrosia still;
When round the very marble of the tombs
The vine's luxuriant tendrils gaily twined
Beneath the Grecian chisel; when, amid
Ionian dancing-girls, Anacreon,
Whose hoary locks were still with flowers crowned,
Could call on Love to fill his empty cup,
And smiled at Death's approach? And whether nought
Still lingers of those times, why dost thou now
Ask me, O bell, to say? Have I perchance
Not breathed the breezes of these riper times?
And having quickened in those breezes new
My strength of thought, have I perchance retained
Ingenuous creeds, that to thy wailing sound
I thus should yield? The sky is leaden grey;
The air is cold and damp; and now the bell,
Which seemed of late so mournful, sends me notes
That sound more like a menace than a plaint.
Perhaps, O bell, thou art that Prophetess
Most terrible of Endor, who appeared
Within the tent of Saul. And why dost thou
Thus call away my pensive mind from these
Severest studies? What a deal of woe
And of despair did he who fashioned thee
Mix with the molten bronze, when it was poured
Into the noble mould! Oh arm my heart,
Thou holy pride of Thought! I am not one
To yield to mystic apprehensions, fit
For foolish women! Let us hail life's strong
Impulsive forces; and with a judgment cold,

As upon Life, so will I think on Death,
Th' eternal law of all that is. I, too,
Revere and love the dead; but now I shrink
In horror from thy funeral lament,
O thou that speak'st from buried centuries,
Thou brazen voice between the earth and sky !

A Butterfly? Into my room to-day,
To seek a refuge from the wintry chill,
Thou cam'st, O little Butterfly; and now
Thou beatest 'gainst the window to get out,
And dropp'st exhausted on the floor; and then
Thy wings thou spreadest, and a hundred times
Renew'st the weary game. I let thee out.
Fly to the open air, poor little thing.
But neither flowers, nor a balmy breeze,
Nor ray of gladdening sunshine, wilt thou find.
The night is close at hand; the sky is black;
And this November breeze is one that kills.

But that lugubrious knell, ah, pauses not !
Its hateful sound is crushing me. Oh let
My faithful muse now help me ! Let her now
Again intone the thrice-blessed hymn of life ;
With dewy roses let us wreathe the lyre—
But ah, the cords no harmony emit
Beneath my fingers now.—Then let some book
As cheerful as sweet April and the morn
Recruit my spirit ; let old Homer show
Where lie the happy island and the home
Of golden-haired Calypso ; or once more
I'll with Astolfo traverse seas and lands
Upon the Hippogriff's immortal wings ! . . .

Alas, the anguish which o'erfills my heart
Extinguishes that sunny poetry,
And while the eye is moving o'er the page,
The mind is far away! In other books
Then let me seek the note of woe instead,
That it may drown that bell's ill-omened sound
Within my soul. But oh how cold, how cold,
Beside the truth of that persisting knell,
Appears the truth of art! I throw away
The book, in which all woe seems weak and limp,
Compared with that deep trouble which has found
A home within my heart. In science, then,
Let me seek refuge; in statistics bare,
In icy figures. O ye lengthy rows
Of figures mute, I call on you to solve
The riddle of the future; ye who tell
This age's greatness, and its boundless vice!
Let me, in you engrossed, shudder at none
But living woes; and may I see, unscathed,
From out the struggles of these present days,
A happier Europe of the future rise!

But ever louder grows the tolling now,
And hurries me away through lonely vaults;
Through the long cloisters of monastic homes;
Through great cathedrals, where the gloom instils
Vague awe into the mind; through crumbling crypts
And chapels of old battlemented keeps,
Where ladies fair and troubadours no more,
But owls, abide. Of hooded penitents
It tells a tale, upon whose brow austere
The meagre mountain-herbs and stinted bread,
And long and ardent ecstasies, as well

As the dull chanting of the vigil nights,
Had deepest furrows prematurely pressed,
And pallor as of death.   It speaks to me
Of ancient shrines, where many a prayer was said;
And pointed niches with an azure ground,
Where, with their heads bewreathed with starry crowns
There stood Madonnas, half concealed behind
A cloud of incense; where, with trustful heart,
Old folk infirm, whose years were nearly spent,
Hung votive gifts.   It shows me ancient tombs,
On which lay stretched full length, still all arrayed
In coats of mail, and with their folded hands
Upon their breasts, statues of fearless knights,
Of which our forefathers' rude art enhanced
The solemn majesty.   It brings to me
A long deep echo, as of clods of earth
That fall on endless coffins; and it cries
With a distinct and almost human voice:
" A vanity, a vanity, is each
And every offspring of the Ages proud;"
And howls and thunders that a grave awaits
Each thing most holy and most dearly loved!

But scarce has paused the mournful sound awhile,
When other knells, more faint but not less sad,
Come from the many villages that make
The lake so smiling under limpid skies.
They float across the heavy drizzly air,   .
Over the waters' ample bosom borne,
Which seems to utter, from a secret pain,
A wide-extending plaint.   And, from the midst
Of the thick pine-trees of my garden, now
A twittering of sparrows rises up,

Which tells me that the last hour of the day
Is vanishing away. Oh hear how blithe
Is that small flock which 'mid the boughs has sought
Its night's repose ! A sudden sense of life—
But ah, too fleeting !—now awakes again
Within my heart : and the departing sun,
Upon the furthest confine of the West,
Meanwhile doth send a colourless farewell ;
Into the room I sit in, through the pane
Which at another season used to flush
With glorious sunset fires. And from afar,
Mixed with the knell, still louder now resumed,
Alternate voices reach me which sustain
A strangly mournful chant. It is the prayer
Which man, all trembling at his littleness,
Sends up to those who, crowned in Heaven above,
May for the many many souls in pain
Pray with more hope than those who still are clad
In our unworthy flesh. There is a faith
Breathed in this chant ; the spirit seems resigned
To a severe decree replete with pain,
Whose justice it admits. And, with my mind,
I see, the while, defiling from afar,
Old men all bent, and boys, and men whose brows,
Manly and grave, were o'er the furrow bronzed
By many a summer sun ; and then a troop
Of women with their infants in their arms,
And leading other children ; and a gate
Opens before them, and they enter all
Into a field of crosses. . . . Suddenly
I bow my face, and hide it in my hands,
And my heart's tempest finds a vent at last
In silent tears. A sudden tenderness

Has o'er me come, together with a fear
Unknown to me before.   Oh, o'er the few
Whose presence makes my barren life to bloom,
Ne'er may that knell, ne'er may that chant, rise up,
So long as thou shalt in my bosom beat,
O my poor heart, O too self-conscious heart !

'Tis the remembrance of the dead, and 'tis
The death of Nature.   But, when April comes,
A mighty wave of life will bubble up
From the deep rootlets of the naked plants,
And run through barky fibres, and produce
A very mirth of green.   I hear the hymn
Of woods, of vineyards, and of hedges sweet,
Of crops and meadows, and a harmony
Of many tints, of many pungent scents,
Of humming bees, of gently rustling leaves,
And tuneful nests of birds.   And I plunge deep
My soul and senses in that mighty life,
And live again for joy !   O ye who lie
Within the silence of the dusky grave,
Say, have the dead an April ?   Wondrous things
Does Faith profess ; and Science tells us—nought.

How many have gone down by different paths
Into the tomb's chill bed ; how many tombs
Of nations, too, have passed away, beneath
The suns and winters, or beneath the feet
Of other younger nations who, amid
Alternate war and revelry, moved on
To History's first bounds !   Alas, alas,
To think of all the joy and all the woe,

Which, since the dawning of the human race,
Have, infinite and fated, swept across
This ample earth, on which we too now pass,
Mere pilgrims of a day! Myriads who now
Have reached those sunless wastes whence never more
'Tis granted to return; the silent ghosts,
Evoked at moments by the intellect,
But in whose veins the living blood once rushed
Impetuously on. Upon those dead
'Tis well to ponder long; but most of all,
Deep in the heart, to dwell upon the few
Who, by our side, around the quiet hearth
Once spent their days. Oh ponder on the dear
And honoured snowy locks,—the infant's eyes,
So full of life, that seemed to mirror Heaven,—
The youth's brave ardent spirit,—or the soft
And modest tresses,—which one fatal hour
Has snatched away for ever! Let us next,
With solemn love, look back upon the Dead,
Upon the men who onwards led our race
To nobler shores. And bowing down before
Primeval sepulchres and new-made graves,
Before the ancient and the recent mould,
Then let us in a single long embrace,
Both kin and friend enfold. Ye virgin souls,
Ye upon whom ne'er fell a single seed
That was not all consistent with the Faith
Held by your timid mothers,—and not less
Ye other souls, with thought's long struggles worn,
Ye who in certainty immutable
Have safe asylum found,—oh, t'wards the Cross
Extend your arms! And ye who on that Cross

See a mere man, but have not yet denied
In Heaven above the presence of a God,
Now, from the heart's remotest depths, oh breathe
A prayer for all these dead!   And ye who cry
That by blind laws the universe pursues
Eternal alternations,—ye, the bold
Explorers of the Cosmos,—oh recall
Ye, too, these dead!   If to the sightless All
They wholly have returned,[1] oh let them live
A second life in your remembering hearts!
Give thought unto the dead, O ye who still
Can hail the sunlight!   Shame upon the man
Who ever should their memory despise!

But night has closed around me unperceived;
And not the radiance of a lonely star
Shines through the gloom; while the adjacent hills,
Of doubtful shape, are looming darker still
Than the surrounding darkness.   Colder, too,
Blows the November breeze, and bears away,
Far from the branches, many withered leaves
Which whirl upon the ground.   Now that the voice
Of the funereal bell is heard no more,
The stillness all pervades.   All hail to thee,
Thou deep, austere, and wholly silent Night!
Oh, dear to me the gloom!   Nor would I now
Break in upon it with the paltry flame

---

[1] *I.e.*, if the dead have been made one with Nature, to use
Shelley's expression.   Also compare the lines—

> " A mighty Spirit had passed away
> To breathless Nature's dark abyss."

Which man from out the elements has snatched.
Such darkness as the tomb's. And so my thoughts,
Just like the clouds which through the inky sky
Are hurried by the north wind's chilly breath,
Make mighty journeys, while within my heart
The boundless light of Love already dawns.

THE END.

www.ingramcontent.com/pod-product-compliance
Lightning Source LLC
Chambersburg PA
CBHW032011060726
47497CB00017B/2966